The Dark Side of Me

Barbara Neveau

Books by Barbara Neveau

Cemetery of the Lost
Folks Called Her Sadie
Jessie's Flight to Freedom
Gentle Is The Rain
The Dark Side of Me

Copyright © 2008 by Barbara Neveau
First Edition

All rights reserved. No part of this book shall be reproduced, stored in a retrieval system, or transmitted by any means without written permission from the author.

Printed in the United States of America
by: InstantPublisher.com

ISBN: 978-1-60458-287-1

All characters appearing in this work are fictitious.
Any resemblance to real persons, living or dead is purely coincidental.

ISBN-3212

Table of Contents

Sharron's Luck

April May

The Bargain

Hoochie

A Child Called Orange

Me and My Shadow

Sweet Boy

Sharron's Luck

    Staring at the night sky with unseeing eyes, Sharron fondled the bottle. That full bottle of sleeping pills had lain in the pocket of her satin robe for hours. The traffic sounds below the balcony were muted by the pounding of her racing heart. The small plastic vessel that contained relief had bumped her leg with every step she took, reminding her of sleepless nights and empty days. Her once beautiful face was now void of any emotion.

    Thomas Lee Schofield watched the golden woman again this evening. *What is she staring at? What in hell is she thinking about that makes her look so pitiful?* He ached to have her confide in him, but he was a stranger.

Sharron Lynn Olson had done it all. Once a much sought after model she had lived life to the fullest. There wasn't anything she wouldn't do. If she enjoyed the experience it was repeated until it became tedious. The world had been her stage and she had played it to the hilt.

Thomas Lee Schofield never took chances. His life was on a rigid schedule and any deviation from the normal caused him fear and discomfort. But he longed to touch the women, hold her and make love to her, if only he had the nerve.

Clarence Fox (Foxy) also watched the woman. *Nice piece, too bad we ain't friends. This guy would have her inside and in bed so fast her head would swim. Gotta meet that broad somehow cause she's in for a good time when she gets to know me.*

The pill bottle felt wet from sweat. A gentle breeze twisted the front of her robe exposing shapely limbs clad only in black nylons. She didn't notice.

Thomas Lee Schofield did notice. His heart leaped with joy, his breath came in small gasps, he was mesmerized by the view.

Clarence Fox (Foxy) also saw the display, "Hot damn, she wants me and I'm gonna give her what she wants," he hissed at the fly specked window.

The ringing of the phone broke Sharron's reverie. Walking slowly from the balcony and she made her way to the table, picking up the demanding instrument she listened. "No" was all she said. Replacing the instrument, she resumed her frantic pacing.

Clarence (Foxy) knew when she went inside that this was the invitation he'd been waiting for. Pacing the room in bare feet he stopped in front of the filthy fly dung spattered mirror, he grinned at his pock marked reflection. "Should change the tee shirt, the pits look pretty yellow." Shaking his head he pulled a worn black sweater over the weeks obvious body odor. Slipping into ratty old tennis shoes, he made his way to the stairs, and down to the alley below.

Creeping along the dark passageway Foxy glanced across the street toward the building where she waited.

Thomas Lee Schofield continued to gaze at the building where his dream girl lived. Maybe, one day he would meet her crossing the street or waiting at the curb and he would finally speak to the woman who would someday be the mother of his children.

Sharron's reflection was devoid of all emotion as she swallowed the handful of pills. Placing the glass on the sink she staggered to the rumpled bed and lay
 down, waiting for peace.

Burning fluid erupted from her mouth drenching both her and the bed. Violent tremors attacked every muscle in her body bathing her in an icy perspiration. Terrified and miserable she flung herself off the bed and lay exhausted on the floor.

When Clarence (Foxy) reached the end of the alley he stopped and furtively peeked out into the street checking for late night strollers. He grumbled, "God damn dog lovers make it hard to earn a livin and even harder to have a date. Owners hardly ever see me, but those little crappers always get a whiff and start their yappin."

Thomas Lee Schofield took one more look at the nearly empty street and caught a quick glimpse of a man slinking into the alley across the street. *I probably should call the police, but what would I say , There's a man in the street below and he's acting sneaky. I seen him when I was watching my neighbor women in her apartment. Just your friendly neighborhood peeping tom. No, I think I'd better mind my own business.*

Waking, groggy from the pills and filthy from regurgitation, Sharron never felt more repulsive. "Goddamn failure at everything I do. Even put these sexy black nylons on so I'd look good for the photographers. Those ghouls who always take photos of dead bodies for the damn newspapers. What happens? I puke all over myself and wake up in a puddle of piss. Nobody told me that taking sleeping pills would hurt so much. I thought I would go to sleep and that was that. Course the ones who were successful can't talk about it and the others don't brag about another failure." Violent spasms tore through her gut, ripping screams from a hot agonizing throat. She fainted.

"Oh, shit," cursed Clarence (Foxy) Fox, "This goddamn door is locked. That window looks like a good bet. Easy to break this lock with a switchblade and shah - zam I'm in. Fucking idiots think they can keep me out with hundred-year-old locks."

Thomas Lee Schofield took one last sweet satisfying drag off the Pall Mall and flicked it out into the night. Watching it arc through the black void his eyes came to rest on the window of the golden woman. That's odd lights are still on but no one is moving. When she's home she is usually pacing the floor like a caged lion. Many a night he grew weary just watching her prowl her apartment as though she was being hunted.

Clarence (Foxy) Fox hunched himself through the half open window. Placing his hands flat on the carpet he dug grimy fingernails into the nap while pulling his legs through the wooden frame. Collecting splinters for his efforts was one of the disadvantages of his line of work, but Foxy thought it beat punching a time clock. A shard of wood had penetrated his filthy jeans and ripped a small chunk of flesh from his thigh. A few blood droplets seeped from the tear in his jeans staining the already soiled tan carpet. Wetting his finger with his tongue he scrubbed the stain until it faded from view. "Can't have those dumb cops finding any trace of me."he mumbled. Making his way through the dim hall Clarence (Foxy)found the stairs to the upper part of the building and began to climb.

   Raising her throbbing head Sharron gazed around the room, well at least it wasn't spinning anymore. The pain in her gut had subsided and the nausea was gone. "Can't lay in this, I stink, but first I need a drink." Grabbing the side of the bed, She pulled herself up to a kneeling position and the pain came back, canceling any thoughts of booze. Staggering to the bath room and adjusting the shower, she stepped into the cool torrent. The cleansing ice cold spray hammered her body until she no longer felt anything except the invigorating stream demanding that she live.

Thomas Lee Schofield caught sight of the woman as she made her way out of the bedroom toward what he supposed was the bathroom and she was walking funny. *I wonder if she's drunk? But no, she wasn't drinking anything earlier and to get that drunk she would have to consume a lot. Maybe she's sick. I better go over and see if I can help, but if I do she will know I've been watching her. What the hell can I do anyway? She would probably have me arrested for a peeping tom. I could say I just happened to see her as I had my last cigarette for the day. Better put the package of Pall Malls in my shirt pocket for proof of my lie. Na, the bulge will look like hell on a fresh clean white shirt. I can't believe I'm really going to do this, everybody thinks I'm chicken shit and they're right. I must be on a nicotine high to even consider it.*

The hall was dimly lit but Clarence (Foxy) Fox didn't care, he knew most of these apartment buildings by heart. Hell, he thought, I've stolen from everyone that didn't have a deadbolt lock on their door, but tonight ain't a work night, this here is a rendezvous with a sexy lady, and I'm more than ready.

"Oh, shit," he muttered, "here comes that frowzy old bag of bones from the fifth floor. Good, she's taking the elevator, I hope she don't get a good look at me. She doesn't have a damn thing worth stealing, just that thingy that holds candles, might be gold plated but it ain't worth getting caught for. "

Clarence (Foxy) Fox ducked his head lower, stopped at a door and pretended to insert a key.

When the women disappeared into the open doors of the elevator Foxy decided to change his plans. "I'll just keep to the stairs, the exercise is good for my back muscles and I'll be using em real soon."

"I can't remember when a shower felt so refreshing." Sharron muttered as she reached for the fluffy white towel hanging on the spindle near the shower door. "I'm so hungry I could eat the ass out of a skunk! Well, not really, but I am starving. God, I've never felt so alive!

Maybe almost dying is what it took to make me appreciate life again." In the steamy haze of the mirror Sharron saw her reflection, and there was a vague resemblance to the once lovely girl of long ago. Golden hair, big blue eyes, golden body, tanned just right, always so confidante. "Now there was a broad who knew how to live. She enjoyed every single day. I wonder whatever happened to her. Where in hell did I lose her?"

Clarence (Foxy) Fox crept up the stairs making sure to keep his weight on the sides of the threadbare carpet steps. "These damn things creak anyway, just not as loud as when you go up the middle. The whole lousy building creaks but that's okay cause tonight I got legit business. She did invite me to come and visit didn't she; well at least she sent me signals and I ain't the kind of guy to say no to a invite."

Thomas Lee Schofield brushed back his thinning hair, threw on a sweater and was bent over tying his running shoes when the fear moved in. He had made up his mind to take a chance for once in his life. He'd just go over and tap lightly on her door, if she answered he would explain about the man he had seen creeping around down in the street, tell her that he was concerned about her welfare. If she thought he was a nut case then he would give up and come home where he belonged.

Clarence (Foxy) Fox heard the elevator hum slowly past the third floor and the hair on the back of his neck began to rise. He was remembering that dirty cur of a dog's bite when he had come face to face with it at the last apartment he had robbed. Cold sweat popped out just thinking about it. That little bitch had bitten him on the leg and her teeth marks were still there. How the hell was he supposed to know she had a damn litter of pups in that box he kicked?

"Well golden girl ain't got no dog, so I'm pretty safe there. Just two more floors and I get my ashes hauled. Been too long, gotta get me a steady girl so I don't have to work this hard for a little romance."

Thomas Lee Schofield entered the elevator located just outside his third floor apartment, punched the button that would take him to the ground floor, leaning against the rear wall waiting for the door to clang shut when he heard someone shout, "Hold that elevator I'll be right there." He didn't relish the idea of sharing the ride with anyone at this time of night but what choice did he have? He could pretend he didn't hear them and let the door close but that wouldn't be right and Thomas always wanted to do the right thing. So it made him a little late getting over to her apartment, it wasn't as though she was expecting him. He was just your friendly peeping tom on a mission of good will.

Sharron wrapped herself in the soft fluffy towel and strode into the bedroom just as the knob turned and Mrs. Goldman stepped into her living room and called out, "Hi honey, just stopped in to see if you were alright. You haven't been out of this apartment for days and I have been worried. I hope you are eating right. I'm making homemade soup and I'll bring you some if you like."

"Thank you Mrs. Goldman, I have been a little under the weather but I'm fine now. That homemade soup sounds real good." Sharron smiled and added, "I'm starved and I'm too tired to go out for something."

"Now you lock this door when I leave, it came open easy, too easy," Mrs. Goldman warned.   "You're lucky I wasn't a killer! There are some really bad people out there just waiting to get their hands on innocent women like us. Gotta be careful these days." She muttered as she closed the door and headed for her apartment.

God bless her nosy old soul, she worries about me even when I ignore her most of the time. Sharron felt a wave of warmth steal over her for the old busybody who treats her like she would her long dead daughter. According to Mrs. Goldman, if her daughter

Alice had listened to her she would be alive today. Probably married to a nice Jewish boy, but no she had run off with an Italian piano player. They had both died in a car crash on a lonely country road.

 Thomas Lee Schofield stood holding the elevator door for what seemed like eternity for the couple who said they would be only a moment. He was just about to let the door close of its own volition when two people dashed for the open door. They were holding hands and the bags they carried in their other hand was slamming against their legs as they ran. Their eyes were brimming with good humor. Thomas felt bitter resentment well up as he watched the young lovers enter and the man pushed the down button on the panel.

 "Sorry old boy," Exclaimed the man, "but it seems as though we are forever running off to some god forsaken place in the middle of the night. I would give anything to be a staying at home tonight."

 The man doubtless meant it as an apology, but it grated on Thomas' nerves all the same. What the hell did these two know about being stuck in a nowhere job, in a nowhere town with no one who gives a shit? He was probably some war correspondent dashing off to be a frigging hero for his ladylove. We all know that the whole world has to be put on hold for them. Well, maybe tonight Thomas Lee Schofield would be the hero if he can ever get these people to move their ass.

   The girl smiled at Thomas Lee Schofield, and winked wickedly. Setting her bag down she clutched her partner's arm tighter as she stood on tiptoe and kissed his cheek. Digging into her jacket pocket she came up with a cigarette and placed it in the side of her mouth.

   Thomas Lee Schofield stuttered. "You can't smoke in this elevator, it's against the fire code!"

   "Ya, well, just watch me!" She said as she pulled out a Zippo and lit the cigarette with shaking hands. Her grin pissed Thomas off but he kept silent.

Some hero, Thomas Lee Schofield commiserated with his fragile ego, *can't even prevent a female from polluting my air. This is typical of my whole life. I try to be considerate of others and what do I get? Why in hell am I even in this elevator at 1:00 in the morning going to knock on a stranger's door and ask a stupid question, like, are you all right? Maybe I should just stay on this elevator, go right back up to my place and forget this hero shit.*

Clarence (Foxy) Fox watched as Mrs. Goldman closed golden girl's door and headed for her own apartment. *Now that she's gone I can get down to the business of making this sweet little piece happy.* Knocking lightly Clarence(Foxy) Fox waited for an answer.

"Oh for God's sake, Mrs. Goldman please put the soup down by the door, I'll get it when I'm dressed!" The exasperated Sharron shouted.

Clarence (Foxy) Fox knocked again softly and waited as close to the door as he could get without looking suspicious.

Sharron, who was still wearing only the bath towel, jerked the door open and stood face to face with the ugliest man she had ever seen. The shock of seeing Clarence instead of her neighbor held her paralyzed for a second. Then she went into action, dropping the towel and shoving against the door at the same time. But it was too little, and much too late.

Back in the elevator, Thomas Lee Schofield covered his mouth and pretended to cough. *There, that aught to make her feel guilty. That bitch, she blew her smoke right in my face. Some women don't know how to behave like ladies, and this chick is one. I'll stink to high heaven when I get out of this elevator. I only smoke on my balcony so my clothes won't stink and along comes this bitch and surrounds me with smoke. I wonder if the woman will notice. Maybe the woman in the apartment doesn't need my help after all. Hell no, I'm not going to let this rude couple change my plans, I have finally worked up nerve enough to do something and nothing is going to stop me.*

Clarence (Foxy) Fox was silently thankful that his timing was perfect. She was waiting for him and she was ready, what more could he ask? Course she was playing hard to get and the punches she was throwing were signs that she like it rough, but hey, if that's the way she likes it, so be it.

Sharron thrashed around on the carpet, hitting the beast who was attacking her, but to no avail. He was too strong, but his bad breathe and body odor spurred her on. There was no way he was going to use her while she was still able to fight. Doubling her fist she hit him in the crotch and heard with pleasure the screams that tore out of his throat. His jeans were down around his knees and when he tried to pull away from the woman he went barreling ass over teakettles into the coffee table, shattering the glass surface.

Sharron prayed that someone would hear the noise of breaking glass and come to her rescue.

Thomas Lee Schofield hurriedly got out the elevator and away from the love birds that had pissed him off. Pushing to complete his mission he now entered the woman's building just in time to hear the shattering of glass in the distance.

"Oh, Christ, I'm too late, she did need help and I wasn't there." The elevator was not available so he took the stairs two at a time. Huffing and Puffing he arrived on the third floor just in time to see Clarence (Foxy) Fox grab the naked woman trying to get out the half closed door. Foxy punch her in the throat, she sagged to the floor unconscious.

He slammed the door in Thomas Lee Schofield 's face and slid the bolt, shouting, " This is just a family quarrel, please mind your own business."

Mrs. Goldman, soup tureen in hand, came running from the elevator and heard Clarence's words. "No! No, that's not true she's not married and that man don't even live in this building! I've called the police but they won't get here in time. You gotta do something."

Clarence (Foxy) Fox was furious. That bitch invites me here with her signals and when I get here she treats me like this. Well, I'll show her, I'll take what she offered and she can't stop me. I'll show her about playing hard to get, even if she wants more, I won't give it to her.

Thomas Lee Schofield, shaking with anger and fear was thinking, that damn old women had to be here so I can't leave. I'm forced to do something, but what? Hey, that rude couple are coming up the stairs. The ones I thought were newly weds. They're flashing badges! "What the hell are you doing here? What do you mean you've been waiting for this to happen? You're what? Your detectives! This man is wanted for other rapes, well what do you know? Sure I'll let you handle it, I don't want to be involved."

Mrs. Goldman looked after the retreating Thomas Lee Schofield and spit out, "Damn coward."

"Cops, stay where you are," They shouted as they smashed the door into splinters just as Clarence (Foxy) Fox finished his copulation with the unconscious woman. Pants still at half-mast he was an easy target. Grinning he held out his wrists to the male detective. "You'll be sorry when she wakes up, she'll tell you we had a date and she got carried away. She really likes to play rough!"

Thomas Lee Schofield congratulated himself on not getting involved in a sordid sex crime. He shook off the feeling that maybe, just maybe he could have saved a wonderful woman in distress.

Sharron woke with people standing in her apartment, she was covered with a vomit covered blanket, she felt icy cold and dirty. Why won't this feeling of filth ever go away?

The cool shower was exactly what Thomas Lee Schofield had needed to clear his mind and relax his body. The Pall Malls his friend Terri had left on the coffee table called out to him and he gave in. Until today he hadn't felt this overwhelming urge to smoke. It had been three years since he quit. Just one more he promised himself, just one more, as he lit it and walked out onto the terrace.

Sharron stared around her empty apartment, everyone was gone and still she had the feeling that the place was full of eyes. Shaking off the eerie sense of being watched, she went into the bedroom to get dressed. She had promised the female detective that she would come down and press charges against her attacker.
    As Sharron pulled the slinky black dress over her head, she felt two soft hands on her breast. Terror streaked though her whole body, What in the hell was going on, the attacker was gone wasn't he? Who could this be touching her this way.

    The detective held her dress locked above her head while he repeated the the rape that the captured attacker had just finished. When he was done using her, he walked out the door leaving her defeated, frightened, and abandoned. She had recognized the detective's voice and knew she had no refuge from the callus arm of the law. Who could she turn to now?

    Finishing the job of dressing, she grabbed a cigarette and walked out on to the balcony, lit it and stared across the street at the window where he lived. He was so handsome that she had constantly yearned for his touch. She had teased him and enticed him with her actions and still he hadn't come to her rescue.

Friends had invited her to the many parties that were given around the holidays but she always refused, she wanted to stay home and pretend the man in the apartment across the street had plans and she was included. She had let him watch her eat breakfast each day, dress for dates, even change for bedtime and still he wasn't interested. "I guess I'm just not his cup of tea. Maybe I've been around too much for his taste. Well that pretty much settles it," she whispered as she flung the cigarette and herself off the balcony and onto the hard black street.

Thomas Lee Schofield watched as his fantasy women took a dive to her untimely death. Why did she do it, he asked himself, she was so beautiful and with his help she could have overcome the stigma of being a rape victim. He would have been there for her this time, not like he was before. He should have taken her away from all this heartbreak.

He should probably get in touch with the detectives who were in charge of the investigation. Well, maybe tomorrow he would call. But if he did that they might think he was involved. Better leave things as they are, after all he has a reputation to uphold. The traffic had cleared away and, the ambulance had taken the women's body to God knows where. He was alone again. He lit another cigarette and stared out into the dark cold alley. Maybe another beautiful women would rent the empty apartment and he could start dreaming again.

                The End
                  Ŏ

Did you ever notice that some folks wait for life to find them while other more adventurous folks race out to meet the day anticipating all the wonderful things that can and often do happen,

Are you the one who waits or are you the one who meets life while racing at full tilt?

B.N

April May
Satan has a sister

    The dank, musty smell of rotted vegetation filled her small black world as she lay in a boneless heap. Eyes blindfolded with a filthy rag, hands taped behind her back, listening to the shovels full of wet earth thump, thump, thump on the growing pile. Her heart is close to bursting; her stomach is heaving violently. Dear God, I'm going to choke to death on my own vomit! I didn't come this far in life to end up this way. She knew the end was near and her mind went back to the events that led up to this final humiliation and desecration of April Kowalewski. What a fool she'd been, trusting fate to deliver all the dreams she had demanded from life.

    April was a beautiful baby, with a fair complexion, blond ringlets, dimples that charmed even the hardest heart when she smiled, which was often. She was her parent's pride and joy, much to the chagrin of her older sister, Ruth.

Ruth was just the opposite of April, dark hair, swarthy complexion, and dark, hard as stone eyes that looked right through you. Ruth rarely smiled and most people found a reason to leave the room when she entered.

Mama dressed the girls just alike so the neighbors couldn't say she was partial to April. What looked adorable on petite little April looked stupid on her older sister and Ruth silently wished that she were dead.

She'd rather be dead than look like an over stuffed version of that, 'little doll April.'

Her days were misery, one on top of the other and had been that way ever since that, 'little Angel,' was born.

At birth, April wasn't red like other babies, her pale skin and great, wide, blue eyes were the talk of the nurse's station on the 3rd floor. People came from other floors just to see the, 'little Angel' born on Easter Sunday. People were always congratulating Fred and Martha Kowalewski on their beautiful little girl, and then they would look at Ruth, stutter and add, err, "both of your little girls."

At first Ruth was happy to see her little sister and proud that she was so different. She soon learned to rue the day the baby came home from the hospital. People came from morning till night to see the baby and cast sidelong looks at her, wondering what was wrong with her. Why didn't she look more like her parents and little sister?

As April grew older she began to realize what was happening to Ruth, her sister had retreated into a hard shell of rudeness and anger, people shied away from her when ever possible. April seemed to go out of her way for Ruth, which made it even worse. "It's not my fault she isn't pretty but I can be there for her if she needs me," she told her parents.

Hate virtually oozed from Ruth's whole body. She silently raged at God, her parents, and the world whenever she felt she was pushed aside or ignored. Her childhood was spent planning on how to get even. "First," she vowed, "I will get rid of April, then I will show the rest of these assholes what it's like to be shoved aside for a pretty face, I will become famous and I won't give em the sweat off my ass even if their dying of thirst.

They will all be sorry."

April breezed through high school and planned to attend college right here in town, that way she could save the cost of living in a dorm. She and her girlfriends were all in a tizzy about starting classes in the fall, but for now they had their whole summer ahead of them. She manipulated her friends into including Ruth in their plans, but somehow it just never worked out.

Ruth smiled on the out side all the while seething on the inside. She thought about her long awaited plan to eliminate April from her life. There was just one holdup, finding the right jerk to help her with her plan.

The boys around here seemed to look right through her just like everyone else, except for Jason Roberts; he was the only one that Ruth could talk to. He seemed understand how alone and rejected Ruth felt. True she didn't really like or trust him but what choice did she have? He was a social outcast with the other young people just like her, which put him on top in Ruth's estimation.

His long greasy hair, emaciated frame and yellow teeth did nothing to endear him to the crowd; in fact the two of them could have been identical twins except for the difference in weight. Ruth out weighed him by a hundred pounds.

Jason was the first to suggest that she start making life unpleasant for her sister at work. Ruth and April had both taken jobs at the local theater in town and of course April sold the candy and popcorn, while Ruth cleaned up the mess in the theater between shows. "Goddamn slobs," she fumed, "why in hell can't they eat at home instead of coming and leaving their mess here for me to clean up. That bitch don't have to clean up after these shit heels, little, ole Ruthie, can do that dirty job, while April stands out in front and looks pretty. Well, someday soon they will see how pretty she is with her face smashed in!"

Ruth began secretly salting the butter so that when April salted the popcorn it had a double dose. The moviegoers began complaining to the manager, he reprimanded April in front of the crowd, and left when she began to cry.

"I can't afford to waste all that popcorn, I'm gonna have to dock you for it."

April had never before felt so humiliated,

she not only had the riot act read to her but she also lost a week's wages. She didn't' understand what was happening, but she knew she didn't like the feeling of being out of favor.

   That Jason is a jerk but I like his ideas, Ruth mused. Christ, he even mentioned once that he wants to start being my boyfriend. I don't want anything to do with that idea, but he's the only one who hates April as much as I do. I don't blame her for refusing to date him, he's a little weird but that works for me.

   I won't let him get a hold on me like he did his last girl, what was her name? Oh yes, Dorothy, Dottie for short. The really funny part is she did end up short, she lost her head over Jason, Ruth chuckled. The police did suspect him of killing her but they never could prove it. The odd part is that the week before she died he had sworn she would never laugh at him again. It would be pretty hard to do that with no head. The stupid bitch, why did she ever start going out with him when she knew how dangerous he was. It not as though she had any street smarts, just hot pants.

   Dad says Jason is dangerous when he's

crossed and that's why he doesn't want me to hang with him. Well, she thought, I can handle Jason! Dad can go to hell! What does that old fart know about living, he works all week and sleeps all weekend. Oh ya, bowling on Friday night. That's his whole life.

    The whole summer was a total disaster for April, everything that could go wrong, did. The salty popcorn was just the beginning, and then there was the wrecked fender that appeared on the car when it was parked in the garage. April swore that she had not hit anything while she was driving and it was fine when she parked it. Dad said she must have bumped something and didn't realize it or she just thought she could get away with this lie. April had never been accused of anything before and she broke down in shattering sobs, swearing that she was innocent of this latest calamity. Mother's clothes being scattered and shredded was the last straw. April being the only one home that day and swearing she didn't see a thing. She had taken a short nap and when she woke the mess was everywhere. Shaking and crying she called the police to report the incident.

    After searching the entire house they

could not find anywhere that an intruder had forced his way in. "Must be an inside job," the officer told her father.

Her life was becoming a nightmare! Dark rings began to show up under her eyes from sleepless nights, but they only made her look even lovelier, more vulnerable.

"God damn it, do I have to kill her before she stops growing better looking?" cursed Ruth! The thought became a seed and settled into her decaying mind. It began to put out feelers then roots and finally after months of being fed with the debris from Ruth's demented hate, the thought became a full fledge plan.

She broached the subject one evening when she was having a few beers and doing a little bud with Jason. "What do you think would happen if April would suddenly meet with an accident?" she ask the half-sleeping Jason.

"How the hell do I know, do you think I'm some kinda swami or somethin?" "Why?" He roused himself from his stupor and asked, "You plannin somethin, or jist dreamin?"

"Isn't there somebody you wish wasn't in your life, you know, like dead or something?"

"Sure, there's a lot of people get in my way, but I just push them hard till they move, course that would be a little hard with yer own sister and specially since she's so damn good looking. Everybody thinks the sun comes up cause she says so."

"I thought you were my friend not hers, I need to be able to talk to you and not worry about hearing my words all over town!"

"Don't need ta worry they ain't nobody in this town cept you that I give two hoots in hell for, course ya gotta add my ma to that list, without her key I'd have to look a little harder for my candy.   Course I wouldn't mind a little piece of that April once in a while, that's one hot looking little bitch."

 "That isn't going to happen, you know she doesn't like you and besides I think she's still a virgin!"

"Yer shitting me, still a virgin, what's wrong with those guys she dates, are they fags?"

"Would it surprise you if I told you I was a virgin too?"

"Hell no, that don't surprise me none, but yer not as pretty as yer sister, I figured some lucky bastard made her when she was bout fourteen, ya know, young stuff."

"You're a real bastard, good thing I understand you or you wouldn't have a friend in the world."

"Who gives a shit, I don't need friends, just somebody once in a while for a jump and my world is perfect! Jason smiled his lopsided smile and pointed at Ruth's crotch, that reminds me, one of these days were gonna have ta take care of yer cherry problem."

Ruth said nothing but her mind was a whirlwind of activity, got him thinking about it she rejoiced, now I just got to keep it fresh in that little be-be brain of his until I'm ready.

The spark seemed to have gone out of April's eyes but her friends stuck with her and tried to cheer her up when she was depressed. She had lost her job at the movie theater and was desperately searching for another place of employment so she would have money for school in the fall. Dejected by the turn about in her perfectly planned life, her mind a million miles away from the path she was taking. She was wandering past one of the run down strip joints on the seamy side of town.

The shill in front of the theater was waving

customers in, when he spotted April in the crowd. He grabbed her arm saying, "You're just what the doctor ordered!"

April was so startled that she let the loud, fast talking man shove her through a dark foyer of the building, past a huge dark door that was labeled costumes and into a softly lit, well furnished office.   The fat man sitting behind the desk was busy sorting a pile of papers and seemed unaware of their presence.

"Boss, I jist had ta bring this dolly in for ya ta see, ain't she somethin?   Honey this here is Mr. Sutton, he owns this joint. Be good to him and he'll be good to you."

The man looked up and stared at April for a long time, his eyes traveled up and down her body several times before he spoke. "Young lady did you come here looking for work, or did my overzealous friend here kidnap you out of some convent?"

"I didn't come here for work.   I can't even dance, sing, or anything," stuttered April.

"With your attributes honey you don't have to do anything but stand there and let the customers look.   Have you ever worked in a strip joint before or are you my lucky star?

Do you have any work experience and how old are you?"

"I'm nineteen and I worked in the show down town making popcorn and selling tickets until I got fired."

"You weren't stealing from the till were you?"

"Oh no, I wouldn't do that, I guess I just made a lot of mistakes."

"Well, if you want work you got it, but you got to wear a lot less clothes then you are wearing now. You think you can do that? The pay is based on the crowd you draw, if you're really good you could earn a hundred clams a day."

April debated the offer in her mind, everyone thinks I have changed so much, that I'm not a good, reliable person anymore, I might as well live up to the picture they have of me. I'll take this work and show them I am at least self-supporting.

She almost changed her mind when she saw what she had to wear for her first appearance on stage. The costume was an ice blue g-string and two blue and rose colored pastes to cover her nipples. "I can't do this" she cried, "I have never even worn a bathing suit half as small as this."

"Honey that's up to you but they aren't going to pay to see you in clothes, you're a good looking kid but your body is the drawing card!" Dry washing his hands and patting his hair kept him busy while he talked. "Think it over kid and let me know in a day or two, in the mean time get outa of here so I can get some work done!"

Tony, the shill, led the silent girl out to the side walk and held the door closed for a second while he whispered out of the side of his mouth "Where in hell ya gonna make that kinda dough around here kid, better think it over."

April's thoughts bounced around in her head, should I take this or should I keep looking for work that my parents would approve, of course they haven't seen fit to approve of anything I've done lately. I've worked so hard to make them think I'm the good one that they always think I am. Dad would throw me out of the house if I told him I was a stripper. Maybe I could just work for a few weeks and not let anyone know. It would give me a nice nest egg for school. What am I thinking, could I really get away with that?

A few months ago I wouldn't have even considered something as extreme as this. I've got to protect my reputation for the future. Am I loosing my mind, maybe I did do all those things I'm accused of and can't remember I did them?   She mulled it over for the next few days not even sharing the problem with her loyal friends.   When she came to a decision her load seemed to lighten.   She found herself back at the House of Delights and the shill was the same man that had seized her arm the first time.

He smiled a big crooked smile showing brown, broken teeth, the corners of his mouth were caked with a white substance that made her stomach give a slight heave.

April tried to avoid looking at his face but her eyes were drawn to that hard-featured man who acted as though they were long lost friends.

With her heart pounding, she was led into the owner's office

"Well I'm glad to see your back young lady, I think we can do some very nice business together."   Mr. Sutton, the owner of the House of Delights, rubbed his fat hands together, then brushed his slick black hair back with both hands. April wondered if the grease came off on his hands and that's why he was always rubbing his hands together.

"I need to know what I have to do to earn some money for school, I don't plan on working here all the time, this is just temporary." April explained, "is that all right with you?"

"Ya, that works for me, but you do have to work Friday and Saturday nights from 9:00 until 1:00, then we will see if that works out for both of us. You saw your costume and there are a couple of different one we sometimes ask you to wear, but you get the general idea, Oh Yea, and change yer goddamn name, that pollack name is too long. It would help your tips if you strolled around the stage and flirted with the customers, but that's up to you."

Deciding to call herself April May, with anxiety torturing her every thought, April waited for the weekend to come. Friday came way too soon and she was back stage watching the other girls dress. She was shaking like a leaf. The announcer began the show with one of the seasoned veterans. Then he uttered the scary words "Now for your enjoyment we present April May in her first performance especially for you."

Performance she laughed to herself, half frightened, peeping out from behind a feathered boa, at the rowdy, shouting men. If that's what they call a performance, I can do that and she slid onto the stage.   She couldn't stop her teeth from making small noises as her chin quivered during the first performance.   The leering faces in the audience didn't seem to notice how frightened she was, they kept clapping and shouting for more.   Her second night was just as scary, but she also felt a slight sense of anticipation when she went on stage.   She like feeling special again, it had been a long time since people looked at her that way. When the audience clapped and whistled for more she began to sway slowly with the beat of the drum, casting her eyes skyward she put her hands together in an attitude of prayer and dropped to her knees.   The men in the audience went wild, each one thinking she was praying for him!   She wasn't sure what she was supposed to do now, should she keep on walking seductively or exit the stage as she was instructed.   April decided to make one slow circle around the small stage, reaching the heavy curtains she quickly darted off and into the waiting arms of the owner. "Good job kiddo." Was all he said.

On her third weekend of work, Mr. Sutton took the startled girl by the arm and led her to his office there he sat her in a chair across from his desk, going around the desk he sat down in a huge tufted, black leather armchair. Settling back into the throne like seat he got right to the point. "Young lady we are going to be very good for each other I can see that now, you have what the clients want and I want to make it available for them. We usually pay the girls a percentage of the house receipts but I'm going to take a chance on you. How does $150.00 a night sound?

"It sounds wonderful, better than I ever expected, but remember this is only temporary. I have other plans for my future. I will be able to save a ton of money for school, and even buy a few new clothes. Thank you, thank you!"

"Don't thank me young lady, thank the men in the audience they're the ones that pay your salary. Give them a good show, keep em coming back and you'll be earning every cent I pay you."

Ruth couldn't figure out where April disappeared to every Friday and Saturday night.   She wasn't with her friends at the movies, malt shop, or the Armory.   Where in hell was she going?   She suddenly seemed happy. We can't have that now can we? Come to think of it, I think that bitch has been wearing new clothes lately, not so dowdy as she used to wear, wonder if she has a sugar daddy, nah, she probably just has got a new boyfriend, wonder who!   I gotta find out just what she is up to.   Gotta get that pothead to help me follow her and see what she's doing that makes her so happy and how I can screw it up for her.   I wonder if the rents know what she is up to, she mused.   Ruth had started calling her parents, "The Rents" as her way of showing her disdain for their way of life.

April's parents also noticed her changed behavior and mutually thanked God that she had gotten out of that depressed, destructive, stage.   They had their sweet, lovely daughter back and both were intensely relieved by the change.

Martha, April's mom, was secretly worried about the skeleton in her family closet. She had never told Fred about Aunt Hollie. Too ashamed and frightened that the curse that tainted Hollie might be in the Schmidt family genes. *Best not to think about it,* she thought, *maybe it will go away.*

April began to look forward to her weekends and began to plan what she would do on stage to insure that she would always be in demand as a dancer. She giggled to herself, "A dancer, that's really stretching it, but that's what the audience wants."

Ruth, hiding in the hall outside April's room, heard her sister's words and was confused by them. Dancer, what the hell is she talking about, she ain't no dancer --- or is she? A frown creased her forehead making her look even more hard-featured than usual. She had given up taking care of herself years ago and her neglect became more apparent with each passing year. She no longer bathed every day and her mousy brown hair hung in greasy tangles along side an angry pockmarked face, filled with bitterness.

April on the other hand went around smiling and humming, content with her world. Friends and family enjoyed being in her company, which made Ruth, even more envious.

When April began getting ready for work on this particular Friday evening, Ruth waited outside behind a shrub in the side yard. Jason was stationed half way down the block in his beater van, as he called it, in case April had a secret ride waiting down the street. She did, but not the kind of ride Ruth suspected. One of the girls April worked with promised to pick her up for a couple of weekends until she could arranged transportation.

When it was April's time to appear on stage the crowd roared with anticipation, she had become a favorite of the men who came to watch and dream.

Ruth slunk into the main room of the theater and took a seat in the rear of the pitch-black room.   What the hell did that dink of a shill mean, I'm perverted, what in hell would he call all these assholes sitting around watching something they can't have and paying big bucks for it.   I sure told him where to shit in the buckwheat when he finally got around to letting them sell me a ticket.   What the hell do I care if there ain't no other women in here, that's my business, not his.   If I didn't want to keep this secret I would sue him for discrimination, that would shut his stupid mouth!"

When Ruth seen April stroll out on the stage her mouth dropped open, her mind couldn't believe what her eyes were seeing. Holy shit! Wait until I tell "The rents" about this! Wait, I can't do that, if I tell them what she is up to, I lose my chance to be rid of her forever. Gotta play it cool for a couple more weeks till I come up with a plan.

She heard the shouts and applause for her sister and her anger turned into a burning rage. That bitch always gets accepted wherever she goes, any wonder I hate her with a passion?

The following night she managed to sneak in the stage door in the back of the theater, answering the night watchmen with a rude retort when he questioned her about her reason for being there. "Old bastard," she fumed, "I could be as beautiful as those sluts on stage if I wore a pound of makeup and took of all my clothes!" She hid in a broom closet until the show began and then sneaked out to watch as the performers strolled on stage and did their bit. Each one had a slightly different performance, but they all wore scanty costumes and gyrated their bodies to the rhythm of a slow beating drum.

Jesus Christ I'm beginning to feel kinda horny too, I gotta get out of here, what in hell is wrong with me? When she got past the watchmen and into the alley her mind was already working on the reason she had these feelings. *It's seeing that bitch of a sister up there showing her ass that started it, most of what I felt probably is shame for her behavior. That's got to be it, I never even had these thoughts before, sure as hell I ain't going les!*

She left the theater and headed for Jason's place, her mind spinning a mile a minute, trying to solve this latest happening to her own satisfaction. *That pothead better be home cause I'm gonna find out tonight what these feeling are all about. He just better be in the mood for a little poom tang too.*

It was not the way she wanted to lose her virginity, but she had to find out about these weird urges. Actually she hadn't even thought about loosing her cherry until Jason mentioned it, but now it seemed to be so important, what had triggered her hormones, was it really the women dancing or was she just ready?

Jason never locked his door when he was home so the door opened on the first turn of the knob. He was sprawled on the fallen down sofa that had been rescued from the city dump; his eyes were glazed from his latest hit of coke. He looked like he hadn't bathed in a month, which was probably true, thought Ruth, but what the hell; I don't overdo the bath thing either. The "Rents" are always on my ass about that, among other things.

She squatted on the blue, plastic, milk carton that served as a chair, and stared at the person she had decided to give her innocence to and her stomach began to churn, as she stared at him she realized she hated his guts. He was what all men were, a weak, foolish male, to be used, manipulated, and discarded. She would go to hell before she let that sniveling asshole touch her.

"What?" Shouted Jason, "What the fuck are you staring at, can't a guy relax in his own place with out some broad staring at him like he's a bug? Git yer fat ass outta here if you don't like what you see."

"It's not you," she lied, "it's that bitch of a sister of mine, she's down in hooker town shaking her ass at the strip joint, and loving every minute of it."

"Yer shittin me!   April working at a strip joint, this I gotta see!"

"You keep yer ass away, this is gonna work into my scheme to rid myself of her forever."

"Can't take chances with that little bitch getting suspicious before I find out what's going on" Ruth explained to Jason as they sat in his basement apartment doing coke. Jason's mom paid the rent on his apartment just so she wouldn't have to deal with him in her home. He visited her on her job only when he needed money or a new supply of drugs. The local hospital where she worked wasn't very happy when he showed up for a visit, but she was a dedicated nurse and they had bent the rules just to keep her working. Jason took every advantage when he entered the nurse's lounge, he snooped through rooms and cupboards that were off limits to outsiders, found loopholes in the system that enabled him to steal small amounts of drugs without being caught. Once in a while he stole drugs from sleeping patients. These little extras came in handy when his supplier was in jail or the pump ran dry. He even acted as a mule when his source needed him to deliver to the uptown crowd.

Jason's mind was on the recent trip he had made to see ma. She wanted him to go into treatment for drug dependency, what the hell was she talking about I ain't dependent on drugs, I just likes the high it gives him. He can quit anytime. *Huh? What in hell is that bitch talking about now? Kidnapping who? Oh well, I'll listen and keep my mouth shut till I see how it works for me.*

Ruth had come up with a plan to kidnap her sister, get enough money to leave this burg and never come back. "Tell this burg to kiss my ass on my way out of town," she laughed as she told Jason about her plan.

"What about me? I gotta have some of that cash to dump this burg too, you can't just take all the green and run! Besides I want a piece of that sister of yers first, an I sure hope she's still got her cherry, I wanta break her in right!"

"I don't care what you do to her, she's hurt me enough with her goody two shoes act.

"Come on, don't be such a bitch, you know she is a looker and could get in the movies with her face alone."

"That may be, but that face is gonna end up in a four by six hole solving all my problems."

"Say what?   You ain't gonna kill her are you?   I can't get mixed up in no murder, that ain't my bag."

"Ya right! What ever happened to Dottie? I suppose she ripped her own head off! But no, I'm not gonna kill her, we're gonna dig a hole and put her in it, if she can dig herself out she will live, if she can't, well, I guess you could say she killed herself."

"Where did you git that we shit, what's in it for me besides a piece of tail?"

"I guess I could split the ransom with you, I don't need a hell of a lot of money to make a new start.   Besides it will be worth half to have, "Little Miss Wonderful," out of my life."

"Yer folks got that kind of money to pay a ransom for her?"

"Not really but they can mortgage the house, they're always bragging about that dump being paid for, you'd think they had the world by the ass cause that cracker box is paid for."

"You know what this is gonna do to your

rents, first the money then April gone, dead."

"Yep, and that's just what I want, the two things they love most gone, destroyed, and the best part will be that they will never be sure about April cause there won't be a body."

"When we gonna do it?   I gotta make a few arraignments before we put yer plan in action."

"Not for a couple of weeks, I need time to plan down to the last detail, can't have anything happening to screw it up."

April spent most of her nights studying tapes, her friends thinking she was studying for classes had pleaded with her to stop hitting the books so hard, after all they reasoned you can't get better than all A's, and she was tops in her classes already.

The other girls working at the strip joint with April resented her popularity at first but her winning ways and the increase in business soon changed their minds. Rosie was a veteran on the circuit and she became April's second mother, watching out for her in the theater and instructing her on who and how to treat clients. Her first rule was no dates with the clients, second was never give your right name or phone number, third was never screw around with the boss.

April listened to Rosie's admonitions and replied "That's going to be easy, I don't have any intentions of doing any of those things."

One of the other girls named Star, piped up with "Honey you don't know in this business what you will do next just to survive."

"But I don't plan on being in this business very long that's why I'm getting an education so I can do something constructive with my life. Maybe with a decent education I can find myself a rich husband," she teased.

"That is what I said a thousand years ago, when my name was still Helen, instead of Ecstasy, and I was fresh out of college. The country was in the middle of a recession, there were tons of others looking for work, and teachers were a dime a dozen. In my last year of school I met a man, loved him with all my heart and soon became pregnant. He couldn't be tied down with a wife and child; he still had two more years of medical school, so there I was a single mom, no job and three mouths to feed. Ya, that's right I worked the strip joints and put him through his last two years thinking he would do the right thing.

Boy, was I in for a rude awaking! When he put in for an internship he didn't even tell me, but he applied to a hospital in San Diego. I never heard from him again. The baby, a little boy, died when he was three years old and I couldn't even tell his father. I didn't know how to reach him. I tried the AMA but they told me they couldn't give out that information. I asked them if they would pass on the information to him and the operator that I spoke to shouted back that they were not an answering service! So you see our plans for the future don't always work out."

"Well I'm going to do my best to keep away from men, and finish my education as quickly as possible. This job is helping me do that and I am so grateful to all of you."

"Honey you're earning every cent you make and don't you forget that!

By the way did any of you girls see the creepy women that watched the show last Friday? What a weirdo, creeping around like a sneak thief, I told old John to keep an eye out for her, we don't want her in the dressing room, can't tell what she is up to."

"I didn't see her, what did she look like?" asked April.

"She was an ugly looking bitch, oily brown hair, sallow complexion, heavyset, bordering on fat, dirty black jeans, and a tie-dyed tee shirt."

"It doesn't sound like anyone I know," replied April pensively, "but it sounds like somebody to watch out for.   What do you suppose she wanted?   I mean this isn't exactly the place women come on their night out."   She was hoping beyond hope that it wasn't who she thought it might be.

"Honey there are some really weird people out there, just watch your step." warned Rosie.

April finished dressing, hung her costumes up for Della, the back stage mother, to collect and take to the dry cleaners.   The other girls left, singing out their good nights, and she was alone.   She sat down at one of the dressing tables put her head in her hands and the tears began to fall. All these years of working to build herself into what people thought as a perfect daughter and now it could all be trashed. She suspected the strange woman was her sister Ruth, and April was upset that her sister may have seen her dancing in a strip joint.

She tried to figure out what to say when Ruth confronted her with the truth. She hoped she could persuade Ruth not to tell mom and dad, but she knew there wasn't much chance in that. Ruth seemed to delight in finding fault with everything. Mom, Dad, and all my friends will be devastated, but they need to think that I haven't done anything really bad. Keeping the trust of all her friends and family was important to her future plans. She got up, straightened her shoulders and headed for the door. She might as well go home and face the music.

That very night after he had smoked a couple of joints she told Jason that she had decided to let him take her cherry, "Might as well be you as anybody."

Ruth stared at the floor of Jason's hovel; her mind still in the planning stage of seducing Jason. She didn't know how to get started, should she just take off her clothes or should she try to act sexy. Oh what the hell I'll just tell him what I want, take it or leave it!

"Huh?" Jason turned toward Ruth with a surprised look on his blank face. "What the hell made ya decide that? I can't just hop inta bed with some body; I gotta be in the mood.   Now if April was here I could get in the mood damn fast, but ya gotta work at it first, ya know get Big Johnny ready."

"Forget that, forget I even mentioned it, I'll find somebody that's a little more willing." the rejected Ruth started a slow burn that consumed her whole brain.   That bitch has got to die and I think it better be quick, Ruth raged silently. Now I will go to hell before I let this sniveling asshole touch me.

"Jason, she began, trying to change the subject, I think it is time to put our plan in action, this week-end ought to be the perfect time to take care of April and get you a cherry from at least one of the Kowalewski sisters."

Jason seemed pleased when he heard this and in his drug induced heaven all was working out just as he had planned.   Hell, he didn't want that fat bitch, Ruth, he wanted April and now he was going to get her and the money too.   The Kowalewski sisters would both fit in the hole he planned on digging.

Ruth saw the satisfied smile and gloated to herself, thinks he is too good for me does he, well he can go to hell, when I am finished with him he will be real sorry he didn't co-operate with me when he had the chance.   His ass is grass!

Friday rolled around and Old John was at his post as usual, checking the doors and windows of the theater, making sure every thing was secure for when the dancers got there. He had noticed the back door lock had some bright shiny scratches on the outside and he wanted to make sure nobody could enter with out his knowing it.

"God darn fools ain't satisfied to just watch they gotta try and figure out how ta touch em too."

Ruth took the ransom note and put it in her parent's brightly painted mailbox with the flowers painted on the side. Jason had written just as she had instructed. Christ do the rents have to put their mark on everything, even the mail box. Why does everything they touch have to be so preciously pretty? She muttered to herself about the idiots that go through live trying to make this shit hole of a world pretty. Ruth waited until her father had gotten the mail and then she dropped the note in, this way she was sure they wouldn't find it till Saturday, that would give her plenty of time to carry out her plan.

Jason hadn't given her any trouble when she had asked him to help her dig the hole, he seemed anxious to get started, little did he know he was going to share the hole with his precious April, then we'll see if he can get it up for her.

He was laying off the hard stuff till this caper was over and then he would have the party to end all parties.

He didn't complain about digging the hole extra deep and wide as he too wanted to make the hole nice and wide, so Ruth's fat ass would be sure and fit into her last resting-place.

Too bad about April but he was going to make sure she wasn't as pure as the driven snow when she went to meet her maker, if there is such a thing. He planned to spend the whole day breaking' her in to the joys of lovemaking. No, he didn't love her, but she's gonna love it when he's done with her, he promised himself.

April couldn't believe that Ruth hadn't told her parents about the job and her dancing at the strip joint. Ruth just went through the week with a sly little smile on her face and was actually pleasant for a change. April wanted to ask her sister if that were she at the theater but didn't want to give herself away if the women turned out to be stranger. She was on pins and needles all week, she hadn't done well on one of her tests and was trying to keep her nose to the grindstone in her other classes. She had decided to give her boss at the House of Delights, a two week notice, she just couldn't live like this, all the lies and evasions were taking a heavy toll on the girl. April had other plans for her future.

    When Friday night came, Ruth came into April's room and asked if she would mind Ruth tagging along tonight, she was getting very lonely for her sisters company. April always seemed so busy these days and she missed April's smiling face.

    April was so surprised she could only stammer out, " Well sure, but I didn't think you liked me or my friends."

    Ruth smiled and answered, "Sure I like your friends it's just that they don't like me, but I'm going to try harder to make them like me too, just like you."   All the while thinking, Ya right, I'm gonna bust my ass worrying about what a bunch of little namby pambys think of me!

April felt like biting her tongue, how was she going to get out of the house and get to work without her sister finding out? Ruth had never asked to be with her before and she didn't want to inform her sister now. Maybe I should call in and tell them I can't make it tonight. No, I guess I'll just have to explain to Ruth what I'm doing and hope she will keep my secret. Maybe if we share a secret, she will think I trust her . All I can do is try!

    April took Ruth's hand saying, " Ruth honey, I've something I want to tell you and then if you still want to spend time with me that's great." She pulled her to the bed and they sat down. Looking straight ahead at the dressing table she began to tell her sister how she started working at the strip joint. In the mirror facing the bed April could see her sister's reflection. Ruth was staring at her with such hate that April felt a cold chill course through her whole body.

    Oh God, I shouldn't have told her, now she hates the evil things I'm doing. I should have remembered that she thinks of me as her perfect little sister. She may be ugly and rough, but by God she still has some standards.

When Ruth caught April looking at her in the mirror Ruth's whole countenance changed, her face took on the pious look of a forgiving sister.

The change was so quick that April thought she'd only imagined the look of loathing.   I really couldn't blame my sister for feeling that way, but I really hadn't done anything wrong yet, except strip on stage. I'm still a good girl, just as good as I was before this all happened.

Christ, that fool thinks I care if she shows her body to men, thought Ruth, *I don't care if she shows it to the whole world.   I just want her out of my life!   She's stupid enough to believe that I want to spend time with her, hell, I want her dead. She smiled as she voiced this in her mind.*

"That's alright April, I will keep your secret, in fact Jason is coming over tonight and we will give you a ride to work."

April was relieved that her sister took it so well. Maybe I've misjudged her all these years, I really thought she hated me. I hope she never finds out that I paid my friends to hang out with her, it help my plan and it took some of the pressure off at home.

Ruth rose, went to the door and turned with the widest smile, that April had ever seen. "Don't forget me and Jason will give you a ride when you're ready to leave."

"What a lucky girl I am, parents that love me, friends that care, and now a sister that wants to be closer." April mouthed the words, but her mind conjured up other less angelic thoughts.

Old John had been having some scary thoughts about that woman that had been prowling around. The week it happened he had talked to his old friends at headquarters about the whole episode. They just teased him about being a retired detective and not letting go of the reins. One of the younger detectives threw the old adage, "Once a cop always a cop," when he said he had a hunch about the woman in the strip joint.

"Ya, well those hunches helped me out in a lot of cases," was old John's retort.

"If your that sure of your hunch lets run some checks on all the girls and see what pops up," volunteered John's friend, Peter Brown. Peter was one of the older cops in the precinct, very close to retiring. He too was hungry for the old ways when you run an investigation on hunches and guts. He asked Old John how many girls there was working, and how many were new to the business.

John told him there were three girls that were new, two less than a year, and the other seven had been there for two years or more.

Peter decided to start with the new girls first, writing down their names and address.

John reminded him that this was to be a covert investigation and if Peter would like to be in on it.

"Oh, hell yes, It's like being back in the old days like it used to be, sure feels good!" Was Peter's reply.

"Hell I know what ya mean, these young puppies don't know what a good investigation with only a hunch to go on, is like."

While following Ruth from the theater one Saturday, Peter watched as Ruth entered an apartment that the police had already were aware of. It was the apartment of a known drug dealer, the drug Enforcement Team was just waiting for enough evidence to put him away for a long long time.

That took place on Saturday, by Wednesday Peter was deep into the case with two men volunteering their time to watch

Jason around the clock. It seems that Jason had been delivering drugs to a number of people that the Drug Enforcement Team had been watching, they considered him a small fish in a big pond, but he'd been behaving oddly the last couple of weeks. They had picked up on his odd behavior, "Either he's cleaning himself up or he's up to something, and I'm thinking it's the latter. He just doesn't seem like the type to kick the habit all by himself. I figure if we give him enough rope he'll hang himself."

Old John took the afternoon watches and had seen Ruth enter Jason's place a couple of times. When he told Peter it was the woman that was creeping around the theater, he was informed that she was April's sister.

"Holy Shit, how can two so totally different girls come outta the same family?"

"Don't know," exclaimed Peter, "but if I had a sister that looked like April, and I was as ugly as that sister of hers, I'd say we found our reason for being suspicious, especially since she hangs with a burnout like Jason Roberts. That dip shit is too drugged out to know his ass from a hole in the ground. He'll do anything to maintain his life style, except work."

When Jason got ready to pick up Ruth and April, his hands were shaking and a film of sweat coated his usually dry scaly skin giving him the look of a man with a fever. In truth he was, but it was not just for drugs. Anticipation of the events he had envisioned in his lusting mind had sparked a fire he was sure could only be quenched with the body of April, willingly or not.

Ruth was waiting by the front door when Jason arrived; her parents had gone out for dinner leaving a pot full of stew on the back burner for the girls. Ruth had been too excited to eat, but April loved stew and had two plates full.

Look at that bitch eat, if I ate like that I would weigh a ton, but she don't gain an ounce. God dam her soul! How funny her last meal on this earth is stew, serves her right!

" Come on April, Jason is here and we don't want to keep him waiting."

"Coming, Just need to straighten the seam on my stocking. It's so nice to have some one waiting to drive me to work. Thank you dear sister."

"Thank Jason, he's the one who owns the van."

"Hey April hustle up, I got places to go and things to do," shouted the feverish Jason.

"Sorry to keep you waiting, this is sure nice of you to give me a ride to work. I don't know how I can repay you."

"Oh I'll think of something!" Jason retorted.

Ruth just smiled to herself and hoisted her big butt into the passenger seat.

"Guess you'll have to sit in the back on that milk crate. I tore the back seats out so I could haul more stuff."

April looked around the filthy van and regretted her decision to accept a ride, but she couldn't hurt his feelings by backing out now. She bit her tongue and slid into the garbage-strewn vehicle. Grabbing a milk crate she shuddered, it was slimy with filthy grease and offended her very being. Sitting down she prayed this ride would be over soon. I feel as though I will need a bath when I get to work, she thought as she swayed with the bumps on this unholy ride. Wait, she thought, there shouldn't be bumps in the road they just paved it a month ago.

"Where are you going? I need to be to work in fifteen minutes."

"Oh, just gotta pick up a package out here, only be a minute. You jist sit back and enjoy the ride."

April had never been late for work and she didn't want to start now especially since she was planning to leave in a couple of weeks if her plans worked out. April's back was getting a twinge from sitting straight up on the crate. She looked at her sister and saw that strange look on Ruth's face, a look of carnal gratification played on her countenance. April had seen that look on the faces of the men at the club, but had never seen it on a women's face before .

Pure unadulterated fear shot through her body. Dear God what have I done. Why did I let myself get caught in this situation?

Jason stopped at a run down shack deep in the woods and he and Ruth got out of the van. "Come on outta there we got a surprise for you.

April now knew that these two were going to harm her and pretending she didn't suspect their intentions, she answered "No I don't want a surprise I want to get to work, please take me to the club."

Ruth's face was almost beautiful in its deranged pleasure. "Now bitch, you will find out what it's like to be the ugly, ignored sister. When Jason gets done with you, yer not gonna be so pretty."

Ruth led the way and Jason held April by twisting her arm behind her back and forcing her into the tumble down hovel. "Why are you doing this? What have I done that you should hate me so? I never did think you were ugly, you're my sister and I love you. "

"Quit the bull shit and get inta the shack, we ain't got all day."

"Christ couldn't you find something a little more secure", objected Ruth , "I can see through the boards of this dump."

"Don't need anything better, we ain't gonna be here that long, did ya leave the note?"

"Of course I did, I wouldn't forget the most important part of the plan. Can't get the hell away from this berg without the ransom money."

Jason was trying to tie April to the broken down cot that sat in the corner of the room, but she was fighting him with every ounce of strength she had.

Ruth watched with sadistic pleasure while the fumbling Jason tried to subdue her sister. Good, he should be worn out from fighting her and then I can handle him with no fight at all.

"Help me git this bitch tied up, I can't handle her alone."

"You're the one that wants to stick her, not me so why should I help, if it were up to me, she'd be dead already."

Jason realized that Ruth was not going to help and if he was to succeed in his plan he would have to win this battle by himself. With a renewed effort he was able to get April tied to the cot but he had used up all his energy subduing the girl.   Throwing himself on the cot along side her, he lay gasping for breath.

That is when Ruth saw her chance and she hit him with a piece of pipe that she had found in the van.   Ruth snickered as she pushed his unconscious body into the garbage laden van.

killed by his own trash. How apropos, trash breeds trash and trash belongs with trash. Christ now I'm waxing poetic, *must be my soft side coming out.*

April couldn't believe her eyes, her sister had killed Jason and she was next. She struggled against the ropes, but they were too tight. Her only chance lay in letting her sister believe she wouldn't fight. She lay still when she heard Ruth came back pretending that she had fainted.

Ruth untied the rope from the cot and wrapped it around her sister's wrist, bending April's arms behind her back she Twisted the rope around April's other wrist then up around her throat, back down to her ankles, there she wrapped the rope around both ankles and tied it extra tight.

Ruth stared at her sister lying trussed up like a calf in a rodeo; she looked so sweet and fragile, even with Jason's blood all over her. *Well that's the last time I will have to look at little, "Miss Innocent,"* she thought as she pulled Aprils body off the cot and dragged it to the van. In the vehicle, she found a filthy oil soaked rag which she twisted into a rope like gag and covered April's mouth so she couldn't cry out on the way to her final resting place.

Peter Brown was furious when he found

out the man he assigned to watch Jason had fallen asleep and missed seeing him leave the house. He was aware that the man had been on duty for forty-eight hours with no sleep but it didn't change the fact that they didn't know where that bastard was, and April hadn't shown up for work. Ruth was missing too, and that scared Peter and Old John more than anything else.

They had been trying to keep everything under cover, but now they had to talk to April's parents and try to find out what was going on.

Peter found the parents having dinner at a local restaurant. They couldn't believe what this stranger was telling them, April a stripper, Jason trying to kidnap her, and Ruth involved in it all.

"Preposterous," shouted April's father, "your trying to tell us that our children are whores and murders, I don't believe it! Come on Martha, let's get out of here, the whole world is going crazy."

 Fred was the one who spotted the letter Ruth had shoved in the brightly painted mailbox. He reached for it with a shaking right hand, but Peter beat him to it. Wait until I make sure we don't smear any prints, he lifted it by its sharp edges, being careful not to touch the flat surfaces."

Peter had followed them home and pushed his way into the house after them.

"What is it?" Screamed Martha, "why is all this happening to us?"

"Mam, we don't know for sure, but this letter may clear up some of the mystery.

"Just as I thought a ransom note!   Well, well, now don't we have a clever little kidnapper on our hands?" Peter read the note aloud, "If you want to see your daughter April again leave fifty thousand dollars in a bag in the last row of seats at the high school athletic field." That sure don't sound like Jason's words, I'm not sure he can even spell athletic, much less use the word."

The Kowalewski were upset having this stranger in their home about to tell them more lies about the children they loved.   How could this man expect us to believe this whole bizarre happening?

"What are we going to do?   We don't have that kind of money; we have a few dollars in the bank but nothing like fifty thousand.   We could mortgage the house, but that takes time. We have got to get our daughter home now, but how?" Fred cried.

Martha pleaded, "who would do this terrible thing, take our daughter and torture us so?"

Peter looked at the distraught woman with disbelief; *didn't she realize that her daughter Ruth was deeply involved in this whole farce? I thought I explained it all to them in the restaurant, where in hell was she when I told them about the whole scheme?*

Old John had made a tour of all the places where young people hung out, looking for Jason's van and asking questions. One couple said they saw the van in the cemetery a while back but they just figured that Jason was there making out with some girl. The girl shuddered when she said this. The boy laughed and explained that it was the favorite place to drink and make out, cops don't bother to check graveyards.

Heading for the cemetery, Old John called Peter on his cell phone and advised Peter to meet him there.

Peter was closer to the cemetery than his caller and with lights turned off he let the car coast through the entrance until it came to a stop.   How in hell am I gonna find them in this dark jungle of tombstones, he asked himself.   Unscrewing the overhead light in his car, he quietly opened the car door slid out, and carefully closed it.   He stood for a moment waiting until his eyes adjusted.   His head said, rush in and save the girl, but caution took over and he knew if he moved too soon he could cost the girl her life. Glancing around he spotted an area that was darker then the rest of the surroundings. Heading for the dark patch he heard the sound of buzzing, low and steady.

She's talking, what the hell is she saying? Wait, I can hear her. She's really lost it now, she's gone and made a song of her hatred for her sister. The more I see of this old world the more I have to wonder what in hell was God thinking when he made man! Shaking his head in disbelief, Peter watched as Ruth continued widening the grave.

"Yer gonna die little sister, yer gonna die and take my pain away, Oh ya!" Ruth repeated it over and over in a weird singsong rhythm, almost a chant.

Peter crept closer and there on the ground lay a dark heap that he was sure was April, but wait there is another dark heap next to her. Who could that be, wait a minute where's Ruth's buddy Jason? *Well I'll be a son-of a bitch! That maniac has killed them both.*

Old John had crept up next to Peter and startled him when he touched Peter's shoulder.

"Christ man you scared the shit out of me!" Peter hissed.

"Sorry, but I thought the whole world heard me coming, It's that quiet here."

"Maybe Ruth's singing covered the noise we made. She's been singing her dreary little song ever since I got here." Answered Peter.

"Looks like we're too late!"

"Let's go, we can worry about that later!"

What is that noise, someone's whispering, did they hear the shoveling and come to investigate. Oh God, I hope that's what I hear, prayed April.

Ruth never heard the two men coming until Peter grabbed her from behind; swinging her around he twisted her right arm behind her back, forcing her to drop the shovel.

Old John bent over the bundle that was April, he checked her pulse and found her still alive. Tearing off the gag he began rubbing her wrists to increase circulation.   She moaned as the blood began to circulate in her numb limbs.   "Thank God, she's still alive," shouted Old John.

"What about Jason, is he still alive?"

"Who the hell cares?" Retorted Old John.

Peter put the handcuffs on Ruth and using his cell phone, called for an ambulance to take the two victims to the hospital.

"What ever made you think you could get away with this crazy scheme?" he asked the irate woman.

"If I hadn't stopped to widen that dam grave you would've never caught me" Ruth screamed.

Old John put his arms around April, trying to sooth her.   She looked pale and frightened but still lovely which made the enraged Ruth even angrier, she fought to break loose and attack the shaking girl.

Peter jerked on the chain of the handcuffs so hard that she was thrown to the ground.

"You hurt me you bastard, you can't treat me like this, I'll sue you for abuse!"

"Be my guest, but if you think anyone's going to listen to a women who tries to murder her own sister, you got another think coming." Peter was so angry he wanted to drag her across the whole cemetery and wait by the gate for the ambulance. He didn't, but he sure was tempted. He pulled her up by the chain that held the cuffs together, bruising both of her wrists and she winced in pain.

"Please don't hurt her," pleaded April, Looking at the two men with humble, downcast eyes she begged, "Ruth couldn't help herself she has always been pushed aside, not on purpose but never the less it had to hurt."

"Oh Jesus Christ," raged Ruth, "now I got that bitch begging mercy for me, I'd rather be dead!"

She pulled loose and took off running, darting around the tombstones like a frightened rabbit. Peter let her get a few yards away and took careful aim, lowering the sights, his intention was to wound her in the leg, she bent low to avoid a tree branch and was hit in the left shoulder. She dropped in her tracks.

The ambulance was just pulling in at that time and stopped where the girl lay bleeding on the ground. Peter ran to where Ruth had fallen, she was rolling around crying and cursing the world in general and him in particular.

With the five people crowded into the only ambulance in town, it screamed its way to the local hospital, where Jason was pronounced DOA, April was given a through checkup, and lastly Ruth went into surgery.

Fred and Martha were there to make sure that both daughters were all right.   Fred blamed himself for the whole mess.   Martha said "No it's both of our faults, if we hadn't made such a fuss about April, Ruth wouldn't have gotten so bitter and jealous."

Peter wanted to tell them that they were blaming themselves for nothing.   He hesitantly ask them if they believed that some people are just born evil, and they responded so vehemently that he let the whole concept drop.   Maybe later they would accept the concept that Ruth was a bad seed, but right now they were too concerned about the well being of both of their daughters.   He had been in this business too long to believe that the actions of good and loving parents can create evil, some people are just born to do evil things, it's in their genes.

The surgery on Ruth lasted well into the morning, as they had to repair a lot of nerve damage to the arm.   She was still unconscious when she came back to her room after surgery and looked so innocent that her parents had a hard time believing this wasn't a dream.

 April had been given a thorough check-up and pronounced physically fit, with just a few scratches from her wrestling match with Jason. She joined her parents in Ruth's hospital room.

A self-effacing April blamed herself for her sister's behavior, and promised her parents that she would help Ruth in anyway she could.

The police guard outside Ruth's door heard the three people talking and wondered why all of these people were trying to take responsibility for the actions of a crazy lady,

He muttered, "Hell, that Ruth girl is nuttier than a fruitcake.".

Ruth lay feigning sleep trying to come up with a plan to get out of this mess she was in and put the blame where it should be, on April!

She moaned and pretended she was just waking, her eyelids flickered just enough to see out.   She watched her parents and April hovering over her bed, dammed sheep, some fool says the hospital is the place where people are supposed to draw closer and these dammed fools will follow the crowd, just like a herd of lemmings.   Well that's alright with me, I can use them again.

"April, April," she moaned, "I'm so sorry this all happened, I don't know what came over me.   That dammed Jason must have given me some drug to make me do such horrible things to my beloved sister."

"Will you listen to the crap that bitch is feeding her family and I think they're buying it," the guard in the hall muttered as he shook his head in utter disbelief.

Martha Kowalewski had that feeling that Ruth was playing games again. No, I must be wrong, she thought, Ruth wouldn't, she couldn't be up to her old tricks, not at a time like this.   Her intuition had always warned her when her oldest daughter was up to no good and she did her very best to run interference in what ever scheme Ruth had going at the moment.   She never mentioned it to Fred because he believed both of his children were perfect.   There were a few times when she was unable to intervene but she knew April was strong enough to survive the childish tricks that her sister thought up.   Martha wished now that she had told Fred about her aunt Hollie, that crazy old lady had tried to kill her whole family.   Hollie had turned on the gas jets in the apartment and went for a walk in the park.   If the woman in the next apartment hadn't owned a dog that woke his master, the whole apartment building would have gone up in flames.

When they asked Hollie why she had done such a thing, she said, "I was tired of looking at their faces and with the money I'd get from their deaths I could afford to move to a better neighborhood."

The judge had sentenced her to fifty years in prison, said he wished he could give her more but that's all the law would allow.   She had been given extensive physiological testing and all declared she was sane.   The final consensus, that she was a psychopath, born with out conscience or the capacity to love.

The Schmidt family was so ashamed of the whole episode that they had moved to another state, never mentioning Aunt Hollie's name again.   Martha was so glad that she could change her name when she married Fred Kowalewski, that was quite a mouthful but it was a long way from Schmidt, thank God!

Now that I think of it, Ruth does resemble Aunt Hollie, a shiver coursed through Martha's body.

Ruth had been watching her mother while acting out her penance role.   That bitch!   She knows, but how?   I've been fooling these idiots for years, why now?

"Come April lets go home," Martha soothed her perfect daughter, "you need your rest. This has been a trying time for you. She paused and stared at her first born, "Your sister needs her rest too."

Fred turned and stared at his wife in shock. "We can't leave Ruth here all by herself, she needs us now more than ever.

"Then you stay, we are going home! Come April."

"Daddy I am awfully tired and my head is pounding, it would be nice to sleep for a little while.   I'm sure Ruth could use the rest too."

Wearing a small sad smile, Ruth told her family to run along home she would catch a little shuteye and see them later. Gotta keep them feeling guilty, she told herself.

The nurse came in just as they were saying goodbye and smiled at the parents. "Here we have a shot to help this young lady sleep, she is going to need her rest." Pulling the IV tube to her side, she injected the fluid into the tube, smiled at Ruth and put the needle in her pocket and left the room.

When Ruth's parents had gone the nurse came back, pulled a chair up to the bed and sat down near the groggy woman on the bed.

"Do you know who I am?" She asked Ruth. "No, well I happen to be Jason's mother, yes I'm the mother who threw him out for doing drugs, but that don't mean I stopped loving him.

He was a lot of things, but he was my son and I can't let his death go unpunished. That shot I gave you will help you sleep all right. Forever. I was telling the truth about you needing your rest because there's a lot of coal needed to keep the fires of hell burning!"

The last thing Ruth saw was the smile on Mrs. Robert's face.

The police ran an investigation and ordered an autopsy, but could find nothing.

They checked the work roster and found that Jason's mother was off on leave. The family couldn't remember what the nurse who gave the shot looked like. As Martha Kowalewski said, "You know how it is, you just expect them to be there, unless you know them they are just another person caring for your child. You don't really look at them."

    Old John had a few ideas of his own, but he wasn't a cop anymore so he didn't feel obliged to submit his suspicions to Peter Brown. His gut told him there was more to this case. Odd how that Ruth died, I wonder if it really was a heart attack. This case could be the something I've been looking for to fill my spare time. I wonder if Peter would like to help me do a back ground on these folks. I have the strangest feeling that we missed something in our investigation. I wouldn't be surprised if we hear from that family again. Sure glad that maniac didn't wipe out her sister, it would've been a sin to waste all that beauty.

    April lay in her bed, exhausted from the stress of this whole episode. Well, she thought it was worth all the effort, all the play-acting, all the ass kissing, pretending to be the good daughter.   Sure Ruth was a pain in the ass and dangerous, but she was stupid and that's why she lost. I get everything! A dose of arsenic given slowly over the next few years should take care of those nosy old busy bodies, The rents.   All I have to do is play it cool for another few years. Mr. Horny Sutton has always had a thing for me. If I pretend to fall in love with him and give him what he wants, I'll have the House of Delights and this house too.   The "rents" and Old Sutton can't live forever.

The End

Ŏ

Do we really know the people who we grew up with? Are they the person we think they are, or are they too hiding another self, one we wouldn't recognize? Look around you you just might catch them in their other self.

B.N.

The Bargain

Jeannie Epstein was terrified when she received the dreaded news. Cancer, what the hell did I do to deserve this? What's going to happen now? Oh god why didn't I check myself more often?   Didn't I want to know, or did I already know I know and refused to face it?

Where in hell is that brave, smart mouthed gal that always knows what to do or say, She asked the mirror that hung in the hall over the phone. Did she desert you when you needed her most?

Putting the phone down with trembling hands, she sat pondering the news the nurse had given her.   She knew she had this sense of urgency lately, as though the world was moving too fast.   Time was slipping away at a rate she couldn't control.   She hated that! Jeannie liked to control every situation.

"God," she prayed, "If you let me make it through this test with flying colors I will give a thousand dollars to the church, or better yet I will donate my stocks to a shelter for the homeless, just let me survive this ordeal."

She went to her computer and began to write a letter to her mother telling her of her fears concerning the outcome of her latest mammogram. Tears slowly slid down her cheeks, her mind wandered back to the time when she really believed in God, well, she still believes, but not really. Not in the God that could perform miracles for his believers, just maybe a Supreme Being out there somewhere that she only talks to when she needs something.

Her friend Joanne believes that everything that happens good or bad happens for a reason, but that is like playing the lotto, either you win or lose in both. Now what kind of God is that? If God is all-powerful why can't he make just good things happen to good people?

"That's exactly what I want to know!" thundered a voice from behind the sofa.

Jennie thought she imagined the voice at first. When she realized that she really had heard it and it was in the same room with her. She shrunk in cold terror.

The voice spoke again, even louder, asking, "What are you willing to do to ensure your test comes out clean?"

A glow lit up a dark corner of the room, the outline of a man was etched in the light, he appeared to shine through the luminescence, as though he was brighter than the sun

"Who are you," she asked, "and why are you in my apartment?"

"I am the Supreme Being and I can grant you any wish you want if you are one of my workers. I am here to help you in this time of uncertainty."

"Ya right! And what do you want from me in return, my soul, well no way little man, this chick ain't gonna buy into that crap, haven't I've got enough trouble already?"

"You were praying for me to answer your prayers and when I do you reject me. Now does that strike you as fair?

"You talking about fair? If you're really God, then you know life isn't fair. You taught me that. I've seen too many good people suffer and too many bad people get away with murder, to really believe that life is fair.

Listen, if you are really God then why do you need my help, if you aren't God then you're the devil and there's no way I'm gonna help you! So bug off!"

"You honestly don't know who I am do you Jeannie? I knew you before you were born and I still watch over you even when you deny me. All I want from you is a promise that you will help the next person who asks for your help."

Jeannie thought for a moment and then retorted, "That seems simple enough. Too simple! What's the catch?"

"No catch, just a little compassion where and when it is needed, is that too hard for you to promise?"

"Well," she answered, "I suppose not, but I still think that is too easy, there must be a catch. OK, I promise I will help the next person that asks, but I better have a clean bill of health for that promise."

"Yes my child, you now are free from the cancer that was beginning to ravage your body, you will live a very long time, maybe too long."

"What do you mean by that, what haven't you told me?"

"You will find out in the coming years, by the way you are much too trusting. I say I'm the Supreme Being and you believe me. I am a prince in my own realm, but by no means supreme. You should have held out for a better deal, good health is easy, quality of life is almost impossible for me to grant."

The ringing of the phone broke the tension in the air, she looked around and the apartment was as it had always been. The dark corner was lit by an antique lamp setting on that precious sideboard that she just had to have. Sure she had bid low, but thats is how you get what you want. She had to own that lovely piece of furniture, even though it broke the desperate seller's heart.

She grabbed the phone and listened to the Dr. Rafferty assistant trying to explain how her test had been mixed up with someone else's. The assistant explained that her name was mixed up with another women named Epstein, and how sorry she and the whole office was. Please forgive them.

"Yea, yea," Jeannie told the caller, "I know

how that can happen when you're incompeteet and underpaid. You will be lucky I don't sue your ass off!"   She said another it was another Epstein, good thing there is a ton of Epstein's in New York. And thank God I don't know any of them except my mother.

    Slamming the phone back into its cradle she looked around and thought the room looked a little brighter.   Well at least he, she, or what ever it was has kept its side of the bargain.

    She dialed her mother's number to give her the good news about the mistake; the phone rang and rang.   That's funny that no one answers, she said she was planing on staying home all day.   Oh well, I will call her later and give her the news.

    The phone rang just as she was going out to pick up a few things from the Deli.   The hell with it, she thought, if it's important they'll call back.

    At the Deli she selected a half pound corned beef, five slices smoked ham, a loaf of rye bread and a German chocolate cake, her mother's favorite.

    I'll surprise Mom, she thought, just make lunch for her; I haven't done that in years.

When she reached the high rise where her Mother lives, an ambulance was parked at the entrance; people were crowed around watching the gurney as the attendants pushed it into the waiting vehicle.

    "Huh, another old critter bit the dust," she muttered under her breath as she made her way to the elevator.   She was just about to press the button for the third floor when one of the old ladies who lives in the building softly touched Jeannie's arm and in a whisper asked why she wasn't going with her mother to the hospital.

    Cold fear invaded her mind. That was Mother on the gurney and I didn't even know it. What could have happened between the time I talked to her and now?   She didn't even mention that she wasn't feeling well. A creeping dread spread through Jeannie's whole body, is this what that apparition was talking about, did it mean I will live a long time, but all my loved ones will die, and I will be all alone?

    Pushing the paper sack of groceries into the little old woman's arms, Jeannie ran for the ambulance.   Banging on the closed doors of the cab, and waving at the attendant, She clasp her hands in a prayer like attitude, silently pleading with the startled driver.

He hesitated a second, then drove away leaving her confused and frantic.

Hailing a cab she told the driver to follow that ambulance and don't waste time stopping for lights.

"Lady you might want to risk your life in traffic, but I've got a wife and three kids depending on me and I ain't gonna take a chance on the whim of a stranger."

"I'll give you twenty bucks if you beat the ambulance to the hospital."

"Twenty bucks won't feed my family if I get hurt or killed, so quit bugging me. We're almost there."

When they arrived at the hospital, nurses and attendants were pushing the gurney through the wide open doors of the emergency entrance. She threw some bills at the cabbie and dashed into the building. She was halted by an attendant holding a clipboard and a pen.

"Are you a member of the patient's family?" Seeing her nod he continued "Please fill out this form and give it to the gal at the in cashier's window."

Jeannie shouted at the matronly women behind the desk. "My mother is maybe dying and you want me to worry about the bill. See me after you help mom!

"I realize you are upset but there are procedures we must go through to get your mother admitted." The pushy little women was shoving papers at Jeannie Epstein. "If you will just calm down we can get this part of the procedure done and it will exacerbate her admittance."

"Who the hell do you think your talking to, some idiot, exacerbate indeed. Why in hell can't you say you plan on making this admittance as hellish as possible?" Jeannie Epstein stared at the flustered, red faced women. "Do you even know what exacerbate means or is it just a word you heard, and use to make yourself feel important?"

The women sat down at her desk and completely ignored Jeannie Epstein. An enraged Jeannie stomped over to the desk and grabbed the nurse by her shirt front. When the orderly came out to check the papers for the permission to treat Mrs. Epstein, he found a frantic daughter and a sullen nurse standing toe to toe.

"What the hell is going on?" The orderly grabbed Jeannie's arm saying, "this ain't no place to tangle ass. Take yourself outside and let us help our patient. We can't do our job if we have to fight the patient's family."

"Alright I'll wait outside, but I will also be speaking to your superior! Haven't you ever heard, the customer is always right?"

"Yes mam, I've heard that, but I also heard that you should never bite the hand that feeds you!" The women at the desk turned back toward the filing shelf and began searching through records.

"Bitch!" Jeannie spit out as she searched for a seat in the waiting room. Can't sit next to that ugly old fart who keeps wringing his hands like he's washing up. Wonder what he did that makes him feel so dirty. That old crone rocking back and forth looks just as bad. Hey that good looking guy over in the corner looks clean and friendly, I'll sit with him.

Jeannie walked over to where the young man sat and smiled as she sat down. "My mother is in here and I'm just waiting to see how she is. People in here are pretty rude don't you think?"

"Lady," the young man spit out, " I don't give a shit about your troubles, I got enough of my own."

"Well excuse me," Jeannie hissed indigently, rising quickly she crossed the room and slammed herself into an empty chair near the window. Staring out of the rain streaked window, she went back in time, to a place where happiness was a dish of ice cream at the corner drugstore.

What happened to this town? It used to be a friendly place where folks smiled when you said good morning. Must have started when those god damn Mexicans moved in down in Snake Town. They should have knocked down those dumps years ago. We got out just in time. Mom didn't want to move, didn't want to leave her friends and neighbors. When I told her my job required me to live in a better neighborhood she agreed. It was a small lie but it served the purpose.

Mom never did get the old neighborhood out of her mind, she still went all the way cross town to buy her vegetables, said they weren't as fresh at the supermarket. Hermie, at the butcher shop still saved her favorite cuts of meat, knowing mom would be there every Wed. morning. Damn people wouldn't let her go.

When I moved out of our place to the upscale new condo, she wanted to go back to that dingy old tenement. I convinced her to stay in the high rise until spring, then we would find her a suitable apartment close to the old one where she could still visit her friends. I know she wasn't happy but I was doing what was best for her. After all who wouldn't be happier living in a place where the tenets didn't string their under wear on the patios outside their windows. Where every morning women in curlers shrieked out the latest gossip while they shook the dust from their rugs into the street below.

So lost in thought, Jeannie didn't see the doctor until he was standing in front of her. He was saying that her mother was doing well, but could not speak. There was no brain damage, but she appeared to be in some kind of shock.

"Did your mother have bad news," asked the young doctor.

All Jeannie noticed was his receding hair line,

"Not that I know of," she answered.

"Was she despondent" he asked.

"I don't think so," Jeannie hated to admit that she really didn't know much about her mother's life of late. She had been too busy.

"We can't find anything wrong with her, is this the first time this has happened? Yes, well Don't worry we will discover the cause of her seizures." Clearing his throat he added a small smile and patted her shoulder. "We are running more test but it will be morning before we get the results. You might as well go home now and come back when we have more information."

"I want to see my mother and I want to see her now." Jeannie wasn't going to let some rinky dink doctor with bad hair tell her what to do. He could go to hell, she was running this show.

"Yes, of course you can see your mother," explained the doctor, "she won't recognize you but you can assure yourself that she is holding her own."

Jeannie stared across the room to where the handsome man was sitting and saw the contempt flash across his face.

Ya, well, he can go to hell too. Him and this pansy ass intern. He's got to be an intern cause he's too young to be a doctor, even with his balding head.

Leading the way to the elevator and punching the third floor button, he entered made a sign for her to follow as he regretfully led Jeannie to Mrs. Epstein's room. The doctor was silently evaluating Jeannie's influence on her down trodden mother. He decided that her mama needed a much needed rest from her demanding daughter.

Leaving the elevator, he motioned for his companion to again follow his lead. Waving at the third floor nurse as she made her rounds, he was enjoying this brief feeling of power over this obviously self centered control freak.

The room was painted a soft pink with white louvered shades, a warm rose leather chair sat next to the bed and a landscape picture hung on a nearly bare wall. It was a restful place to sit and wait for Mama while she fought this personal battle with death.

Is this what the ghost, spirit, or what ever the hell he was, meant when he asked what I would be willing to do. Would I take my mama's place? I don't know. I'm young and she's old. I have my whole life before me and she's at the end of hers. She's seen things I will never see, changes I take for granted. Mama has had love and I have never had any love except mother love. I have my whole life waiting for me and I should give it up for an old women who just happens to be my mother. I wonder, what would I do if this were really a test. It couldn't be. it's too soon after his visit, this Supreme Being, angel, devil, or what ever the hell it was, or was it just my imagination. This must have been a coincidence and I've blown it way out of proportion. Too damn much work has got me seeing things where nothing existed.

    Jeannie sat down by the bed and taking her mother's hand, prayed that she would come out of the dream world where her mind was hiding. OK, so Mama needed to be in her own little space even if it was back in that dark rickety apartment where she had loved her husband, raised her family, and wanted to spend the rest of her days on earth. If that is what she wants then so be it.

    "Mama, I'm going now, but I will be back in the morning with a little surprise for you"

    Mama stared back at Jeannie with unseeing eyes.

    Waiting for the elevator, Jeannie stared at

the bare white walls, heard all the sounds that seemed to be shouting at her, get me out of here.

A man in the room across from the elevator lay sleeping under white sterile sheets, tray still covering half of his bed. The low moans coming from the bed hidden by cheesy drapes hanging between the two beds like shower curtains seemed to be the dividing line between life and death.

Tearing her eyes away from the room as the bell rang signaling the arrival of the small square box that would transport her to the main floor, she pushed her way into the crowed conveyance. She hoped no one would brush against her. She hated that feeling of being fondled by strangers. Sure they were all jammed into this box but they could keep their distance from her, after all they were just a bunch of low lives. What kind of a women goes out in public with her hair in rollers and wearing a dirty shirt? Christ, look at that teenager with his pock marked face with slimy ooze seeping out of the red blotches on his ugly little face. And last but not least that old man in the brown stripped trousers and red plaid shirt. He smells like he shit his pants.

While Jeannie was evaluating her companions in the crowd, they were reliving the events that brought them to this place and this time.

Fred Jonas wished that he had listened when Myra complained about her back hurting, but selfish bastard that he is, he had kept on watching the ball game. Dammit he deserved a little recreation on the weekend. Wishing she would stop complaining, he had tried to go back to watching the game, but his mind kept going back to a younger Myra, the times she had flirted and teased him to pry him away from the game. Fred chuckled as he remembered how horny she used to make him. The teasing had always worked back then and her back didn't hurt her a bit even in those kinky positions. Damn those were some good times. Myra always told folks that he chased her till she caught him, and then she'd giggle. After forty seven years that little joke got old, but then so did they. At first Myra had wanted kids but Fred didn't, so they were a couple with no anchors to tie them down. They never went any place or did anything, but they were free to do so if they wanted.

These last few years Fred had some regrets about being childless, but he never told Myra. Now he was facing life without anyone in his life. Friends were either dead or too busy with their families to bother with Fred and Myra, and now the doctor tells him that she has had another heart attack. *Hell, I didn't know she had the first one*. Doc said women often have back aches to signal the attack is coming. They don't always get the stabbing pain that men do. *What in hell am I going to do without her? She's the only one I have to remind me that I need a shower, can't seem to remember much these days, got to get to the doctor and get healthy. Somebody has got to take care of Myra.*

Turk Jamison tore his gaze from that snooty bitch who thought she was such hot shit and stared at the graffiti that was slashed across the wall next to him. He couldn't read all of it but somebody had written a phone number and the words, good time, were still visible. *Good time, that is what he had started out to have tonight. Didn't nobody tell him that the dance would be invaded by a bunch of dudes with a hard on for his friends. They wanted war and thats just what they got. His* piece was laying at the bottom of a sewer in about three feet of water.

I can't believe I shot that bastard, but he asked for it, laying hands on my girl. Pena took one in the arm and Jake got one in the back. I bet that bastard Jake was running at the time. The shit really hit the fan when that black girl was shot, somebody said she was dead. I just had to come and see how my buds are doing and find out about the girl. The cops won't suspect me cause who in their right mind would come to the hospital if they was guilty of anything. Dumb cops!

Diane Russell knew her son was dying. Huffing was the latest thing these dumb kids did to escape their unbearable world and he had done it one to many times . *Goddamn kid was always trouble right from the start. When he was three he had crawled up onto the cupboard and found my birth control pills. God knows how many he ate. Then there was the time he set the house on fire when I was sleeping. He must have been about five that time. So I had had a few friends over the night before, but they left early. That smart ass fire marshal said that having beer bottles all over the living room added to the danger* for his men when they were trying to fight the fire. He said most of the bottles were filled with cigarette butts, but there were some bottles that had exploded. The broken glass was dangerous. Sarcastic asshole said he was surprised that I had slept through the noise of the siren and men chopping down doors. I still don't know why they had to break down the damn doors they weren't locked. Now he pulls this shit again, friggin kid just tries to make my life miserable. If I'd a known which guy was his old man I would have given the kid to him years ago, let the bastard find out what it is like trying to raise a teenager in this day and age. It's time for somebody else to take responsibility for the kid.

    She thinks I didn't see the dirty look that nurse gave me when I told her to call me if there was any change. So I'm not mother of the year I still care about the kid and did my best to raise him right. Sitting by his bed while he slept was not going to make him get better any faster and a gal has got to take a break and get a little libation, maybe some food too. That high tone bitch is staring at the the rollers in my hair and food stains on my blouse. Well a girl is allowed to be a little *shaky when she's getting ready to go to the hospital to see her only son. So I spilled some soup on my shirt, no big deal. She's still staring at my hair. I bet she's jealous cause her hair looks pretty ratty all punched up in wet looking curls. I always did have good hair and I take good care of it. Well, a gal has to take care of herself, she'll never get a man if she lets herself go. I bet that bitch never had a man in her life, thinks she's too good I bet.*

Jeannie decided to leave the hospital and get some decent food at one of the nearby eateries in the neighborhood. Slamming her way out of the main entrance she stepped out into the street. Her thoughts were on her warped perception of hospital food. Running through her mind were these thoughts. *The crap they feed you in the hospital cafeteria is like eating cardboard on a bun. She never saw the bus.* When she next woke, she was in a bed with needles and tubes everywhere. When she tried to speak her mouth wouldn't cooperate, no sound came out of her throat, When she tried to move her legs to sit up they were too heavy to lift. What the hell is going on she asked herself. Why weren't they listening to her groaning and trying to speak?

The doctor and nurses were in the hall discussing her situation and she heard the prognoses. "She is as strong as a horse, her heart is good and there is no internal bleeding but her spine is damaged. She is paralyzed and will never be able to walk or speak. She should live a long, long life. The bad part is her last living relative, her mother, just died. I hope she made a lot of friends in this life because that is all she has left."

These thoughts seeped into Jeannie's empty gut.

I've won or have I ?

The End

Ŏ

What is there to say, she will continue to live as she has lived and no one even cares.

B.N.

Hoochie

"If that bitch was dead my life would be a hell of a lot easier!"

Thomas John Miller, better known to his friends as Hoochie, smiled as he tipped the can of Bud to suck out that very last drop. Budweiser was the nectar that provided forgetfulness for Hoochie.

The escape from that crappy damned job, hell no, oblivion from the crappy damned life. Every morning of the week, numb from a liquid breakfast, he punched into that friggin prison they call a factory, every damned day of every damned month of every God damned year.

Thomas John Miller was the tenth child born to Hilda and Jake Miller. "Christ they should have stopped at nine," was Hoochie's retort to anyone who asked how many children were in his family. He, being only five foot tall, blamed his parents for using up all the growth genes on his 6' 2 inch older sister, and 6' 4 inch older brother, and all the rest of those bastards that were taller then he was. Who in the hell wouldn't be grouchy when you spent most of your life looking up your sister and brothers asses?

Amazing Grace was what T.J. secretly called Grace, his older sister She pretended she was perfect, but T. J. had caught her and Thomas Franks rolling around in her bed when Pops and Mom was out shopping for grub. She was always looking down on me for drinking a few Bud, well so much for her being perfect, and a virgin. To bad she didn't get knocked up!

The gang of guys that he hung with began calling him Hoochie at the tender age of fifteen. That is the age he was when he found out that a drink of hooch for breakfast made his day a lot more bearable. His problems all began when he beat up the older neighbor boy for touching him on the crotch. That incident brought back unpleasant feeling of guilt and shame and he didn't know why.

He didn't remember when he first started hating his miserable life.

Was it when that bitch of a Stella bugged out taking the furniture, the bank account, and the kids? Why she went he'll never know, so he punched her around a little. She must have liked it course she was always asking for it. He didn't really give a shit about the furniture or the money in the bank, but when she took off with his kids she really pissed him off. They were the only good things that had happened in his miserable life. Shauna with her blond curls and angel blue eyes, always sweet natured and smiling. So she wasn't as smart as Tommy John Jr, but she was a hell of a lot easier to live with. That little shit of a Tommy always getting in trouble.

    Hoochie dipped the large metal ladle into the pot of molten metal, scooped up a dipper full and poured it into the gapping cavity on the back of the machine. After pushing the buttons that activated the huge die and stamped out two more rewind starters that were used in the building of lawnmowers, and with a scornful smile he went back to his daydreams.

    That kid has really got a mouth on him, he can swear like a trouper. That priest who brought him home is making mountains out of molehills, Tommy ain't gonna end up in the joint, not if I can help it. So he drank a little of the church's wine, so what? Every kid I know did that. Why it's almost a rite of passage for a Catholic kid to sample the priest's private stock. So what if he pulled up the blouse of the neighbor girl, he was checking to see if she started to bud yet. Hell I did that myself a time or two and I ain't no jailbird. My mother said I was a chip off the ole block, well this chip is a lot smarter than the old man, cause I ain't gonna screw myself out of a life, and screw the kids out of a life too.

When the noon whistle blew Hoochie threw off his face shield and gloves, untied his apron and tossed it onto the inspector's table, headed for the time clock, and punched out. The 'Do Drop Inn,' across the street had his cold Bud waiting just as they have every weekday for the last ten years. If he drank fast he'd have just enough time for two cold ones before he had to punch back in. Tossing down the last drop from the still cold second beer, Hoochie raced back to the plant, slammed through the swinging doors and punched in a minute late, just as he had done for the past two years. Several times Fred the foreman had called him on the carpet for being late but Hoochie always told that bastard where to take his complaint and where to shove it.

They used to be drinking buddies until Fred went and got saved, then joined the Salvation Army. What a joke! That fat bastard couldn't fight his way out of a paper bag and he joins an army. Fred's wife had given him the word, "Quit drinking or we leave?" Hell she was just threatening him and he fell for it. My old lady promised that for years, but she didn't say anything about taking the kids, till now.

After the union rep and Fred cornered him and threatened him with dismissal, he set a smile on his face and pretended to listen to the warning. For two weeks Hoochie made it back from lunch on time. Shaving time from his lunch meant he could only have one Bud, but that was enough to keep the glow going until after he punched out.

Over and over for the last six months his co-workers warned him of his carelessness while pouring the molten metal but he didn't listen. Going back to his die cast machine after lunch, he put on his apron, grabbed his shield, placed it on his head, and reached for his gloves, but they didn't come away from the table where he had thrown them. "What the hell," he cursed as he pulled harder; he still couldn't get them loose. "Some dirty bastard nailed them to the table," he mumbled, "just wait until I find the bastard who did it," he promised the smoke filled air around his machine. Cursing everyone and everything he swore vengeance on the guilty party, "He's going to pay hell for that little stunt."

Thank God it was Friday so he could get the hell out of this hole and away from these smart ass bastards. Sure he had pulled a few of these same tricks when he was younger but that was for fun and only on the dead heads who didn't do their jobs. I don't know why those assholes would pull that shit on me. Hoochie fumed through the next four hours.

There's the quitting buzzer, about frigging time, the days are getting longer and longer. I wonder if somebody's screwing with the clock. It wouldn't surprise me if they took five free minutes every week, which would really add up for a plant that has over three hundred workers. Well I'll show them, I'll screw them out of my five minutes.

    Hoochie hadn't worked a weekend for years, as that was his time to rest and spend time with his family. The bitch and kids were always up before him and made enough racket to wake the dead. She'd always complained when he crawled out at of bed around noon, but what the hell when a man slaves in a shop all week he needs his rest on the weekends.

Sure I always have a few beers before I get home and couple more after I get home, but what the hell a man's gotta have a little recreation. A wife nagging about how much he money spent on booze sure didn't help the situation.

    What the fuck went wrong with his life? He's seen some guys who are happy to punch into that hell hole, slave all day for the few bucks they pay us, then go home to a house full of screaming kids, and think their lucky. Well that ain't me! I know when I'm being screwed and I don't have to roll over and act like I like it.

Stopping at the 'Do Drop Inn,' after punching out of the factory that was using up his life, Hoochie drank until the bartender refused to serve him any more. Chuck, the bartender told him just as he had every Fri for the last ten years, to go home to his wife and family. Chuck called a cab for him and didn't have to tell the cab driver where his drunken customer lived.

    Art the cabby had driven Hoochie home every Fri. for the last three years. Hoochie had lost his license when Stella called the police on him for driving through two fences on his way home from work. The cops roughed him up when they tried to get him out of the car and he couldn't understand why, all he was trying to do was light a cigarette.

    Stumbling out of the cab Hoochie tossed some crumpled up bills at Art and said, "keep the change." Staggering toward the house he glanced around to see how many of the neighbors were watching him come home from a hard days work. Curtains moved but no one showed their face at the window or opened the door. "Screw you chicken shits hiding behind a frigging curtain."

    Hoochie knew he was the talk of the neighborhood, but he didn't care as long as they stayed on their own side of the fence. Waking up in the morning with the usual headache, Hoochie swung his legs over the jerry rigged bed where he had spent the night. Holding his head he tried remembering how he got home. He couldn't recall leaving the bar but he must have because here he was all safe and sound. Those people at the bar sure knew how to take care of me. Hoochie's foggy mind told him, not like that that useless wife and kids. Some people appreciate the hard work and sacrifice that he contributed every day of his miserable life.

    The empty house echoed his grunts as he bent over the old beat up red Coke cooler that was a permanent fixture under his makeshift bed. Grabbing his first beer of the day he cursed his sore back ; a man needs to rest in a decent bed in his own home, not on a God damned hammock. Good thing he'd remembered the air cushion that had survived the pool days, it had been deflated and shoved into the corner of the dilapidated shed. Using the kid's bicycle tire pump he was able to inflate it enough so he wasn't sleeping on that hard tarp that he had used to repair the old hammock

    After drinking his breakfast, he wandered out to his shop in the back of the house. There in the sawdust and cobwebs was the boat he had spent many a year repairing so the family could go on fishing trips. It had been several years since he had even touched it. It stood like a giant replica of his own wasted life. Hoochie complained bitterly to the litter that lay strewn everywhere in the nearly neglected shed. "I'm just as unfinished and abandoned as this piece of shit called a boat. With the bitch gone I'll have a lot of time to work on the boat, I'll show her highness how much time she screwed me out of with her constant nagging about household chores. When I get it finished I'll invite the kids to go on its maiden voyage and won't take the bitch along, I won't even ask her. That'll show her, always bitching that I start something and never finish.

"Better get a beer to wet the whistle, funny how I always get thirsty with sanding. Huh, I thought I finished this part of the sanding along time ago, must have roughened up from the leaking roof. Setting in this damp shed didn't help much either. Maybe I should fix the roof first then get the boat finished. Oh shit, the roof needs new shingles and I'm broke so that settles that, no senses in sanding cause it won't stay smooth as long as it's rained on.

"Ain't that a crock, gotta keep a boat dry so you can put it in water, wouldn't that frost your cookies? Wonder if old Fred wants to come over and help finish the boat when the roof is fixed. Oh shit I forgot, he don't imbibe no more and his old lady don't like his hanging out here. Like I'm gonna pour beer down his throat, he's a grown man and can decide for himself."

Right after Christmas last year, Hoochie, with the inevitable can of beer in hand, had begun having conversations with an invisible someone, even loud verbal arguments while pacing up and down the snow filled driveway.

The neighbors, who couldn't help noticing Hoochie's strange behavior, had cautioned their children to stay away from the Miller house and the Miller children. No sense in taking chances .

Floyd Brown, Hoochie's closet neighbor, even shouted out, "Hey Hoochie, what are you doing, stamping out snow? Stick a shovel in your ass and you'll have your driveway clean in no time!"

Hoochie's face flushed bright red, his eyes grew wild, shouting of obscenities at the offender, and to finish his tirade he threw the empty beer can in the direction of the Brown's house. Those neighbors who were not at work watched with concern, this used to be a nice neighborhood, some commented.

"Fuckers, don't know when to mind their own business, I can walk up and down in my own driveway if I want. Hell, I can have a parade in the god damned driveway if I want to and they can't do a damn thing about it!"

    Hoochie's ranting and raving had begun the fifth year after the wedding to Stella Schmidt, a girl he had met while working at the factory. His courting consisted of taking her to his buddies home where they played cards and drank booze. When his friends tired of his belligerent attitude he began taking her to his favorite bars. Stella could put away a six pack in the same amount of time as Hoochie, but she never got mean or sloppy ass drunk. She had grown up in a house where booze was readily available and she learned at an early age that it gave her a pleasant glow.

    Stella was sure as soon as they were married Hoochie would quit drinking or at least cut down on his consumption, she knew she would cut down or even quit when she got pregnant. The wedding ceremony was short and not so sweet, Hoochie was drunk when he came to the church and picked an argument with the minister over the price of his services. That was Stella's first indication that this marriage was going to take a lot of work. What she didn't consider was Hoochie's all out revolt when she mentioned living married life without booze.

   Houchie's thoughts went back to the first few weeks of their married life. *Me and Stella were quite happy until she went and got herself knocked up, then the kids came one after the other. I put a stop to that in a hurry after the second one. Shauna was retarded and I know it was because the ole lady stopped drinking and started taking that shit the doctor gave her. I had to go to the bar alone after that, so I cut her out of the twice a week roll in the hay. She complained about no more fun in bed and accused me of having some floozy on the side. I didn't have a girl friend, hell I didn't even care if I had a jump or not.*

    That's when the ole lady really began her bullshit, taking the kids to her mother's house all the time so she could run the streets with god knows who. Those sluts she hung around with before we got married are sticking their noses in our business all the time. Just because that bitch Sally married a doctor she thinks she's hot shit. Well she sits down to crap just like I do.

I bet they are the ones that told her to leave when I was at work. Bitches! They don't know how it hurt to come home after busting my ass all day in the shop and find an empty house. That bitch even emptied out all my beer, left the frigging cans in the sink. I bet she's still laughing!

    Hoochie didn't care if it was as the radio announcer had pronounced it the worst storm of the year. He had to get that damned driveway clean so he could get to the store to buy his supply of beer. He could weather the storm if he had enough liquid refreshment. So wrapped up in his own little world was Hoochie that he didn't see the little red Honda that came speeding around the corner. The driver was going much too fast for weather conditions. The build up of ice under the snow covered street made keeping the car under control impossible. When the driver realized that she was losing traction she tried applying the brakes. That was the wrong thing to do on ice and snow and the vehicle was sent into a wild spin, coming to rest on Hoochie's driveway with him underneath. He didn't feel the pain at first, but when he tried to move out from under the car he nearly fainted. He had often experienced a similar dazed condition but not the excruciating pain that came with this collision. The automobile was only slight damaged but Hoochie's leg was bent at a sickening angle. When the ambulance came and a young medical intern examined him. The sympathetic medic explained to the irate Hoochie that his leg was broken in two places.

"Well I ain't going to the frigging hospital, I feel okay, just a little sore," was his answer to the medic. He was watching his language because a crowd of youngsters had gathered to watch the excitement. They think they can put me in that dammed prison of a hospital and keep me from having my daily liquid refreshments. Well, they can't force me to go, I'll stay home from work
for a couple of days and I'll be fine. I'm a tough old bastard. They can't keep me down!

"Sir we can't leave you here," the unsympathetic older medic calmly told Hoochie, "if when you get to the hospital and a emergency doctor checks you out, and you still want to leave then that is up to you. Lets get this man loaded and on our way," the older medic sternly shouted,

Hoochie accepted the fact that he couldn't fight the two medics who were now loading him into the ambulance, but, he thought, wait until I talk to that asshole emergency doctor, I'll show him where the bear shit in the buckwheat!

On the way to the hospital the beer began to wear off and Hoochie's leg was throbbing so fiercely that he could barely keep from screaming. When the pain grew into a fire that was consuming his whole body he began a low moaning cry, then a strangled scream that wiped away all thoughts of being macho.

The high-speed ride in the ambulance had been dangerous and the skids had thrown Hoochie around on the gurney he was strapped to. By the time they reached the hospital that scream was a constant howl. Two nurses had rushed out of the break room to take charge of the bawling patient.

It had been a long day for these dedicated women. They had just finished calming down a young girl who was going into labor for the first time. Their coffee break was way past due and they both were exhausted. There had been another automobile accident earlier, the father had died at the scene, but the mother and child had survived. Both victims had needed operations to put pins in their elbows and legs.

    A shooting at a notorious bar across the river, by person or persons unknown, was another emergency. The victim's homeys had flocked to the waiting room or prowled the halls waiting for the doctor's to finish the surgery. They were loud and rude, scaring the hospital staff so badly that an intern had called the sheriff's office to ask for help. The officer who answered the phone explained that there were so many accidents from the storm that they couldn't get there for a couple of hours. Brave staff that they were, both the doctors and nurses
continued to minister to the sick and wounded.

    Doctor Davis explained to Hoochie that the breaks in his leg were severe enough to cripple him for life if he didn't let them do surgery immediately. By this time the liquid refreshment had worn off completely and Hoochie was ready for anything that would take this pain away.

When the nurse came to take his blood he pitched such a fit that they had to hold him down. After running the blood test the doctor decided not to operate right away and to withhold pain medication until his blood was stable. "I need a drink or something, this pain is killing me."

"Can't do that until we run more labs on you. Doctor left orders that you are not to have anything stronger then aspirin until all the alcohol is out of your system." The smiling woman set a fresh carafe of ice water on his bedside table and suggested he try to sleep and she would contact the doctor in a few hours.

"What the hell do you mean you can't give me anything to take away this pain?

The emergency room was made ready for the next patient and the exhausted doctor directed a nurse to start ivies on an old man who had come in with chest pain. Doctor Davis decided to grab a cup of coffee and a quick smoke to steady his frayed nerves. The dedicated doctor Davis was trying his damnedest to quite that filthy habit but every time he had a night filled with ugliness and pain he reached for another Camel.

After several hours Houchie's blood had stabilized enough to be given pain medication.

The room they wheeled Hoochie into was brightly lit, smelled of disinfectant and he felt his stomach roll. The last thing he remembered before the mask came down was the smell of cigarette smoke on the doctor. *That bastard went out to have a weed while I'm laying here in pain!* He woke himself up moaning,

"Where in hell am I, and why am I crying like a baby?" Then he remembered the accident, the pain, and that bastard of a doctor who went out for a smoke.

"Now who in hell is this?" he muttered. The woman that had entered his room was good looking in a plain sort of way. She may be ugly, but she sure is built like a brick shit house with not a brick out of place.

"Who the hell are you? What the hell do you want, and why in hell are you in my room? Are you a social worker?"

He had expected that bitch of a Stella to sic the government on him along time ago and now when he's down she kicks him!

"My name is Angela White and I'm the one who accidentally hit you," she answered, "I came to apologize for hurting you. And yes, as a matter of fact I am a a social worker. That is my job, but I wasn't working when I hit you, I was going to meet a friend who needs my help. If there is anything I can do to help you please let me know."

"Get the hell outta here, ain't I in enough pain without you rubbing it in?"

Leaving the room she softly whispered, "I will come back tomorrow when you're feeling better."

"Don't bother," shouted Hoochie, "I'm going to sue your ass off, so how about those apples? Your sucking around ain't gonna change a damned thing." *That bitch thinks she can change my mind about suing, well she can't. God how I wish I had a drink! Wonder if the doctor would prescribe it. Hell they could put a hold some of the other drugs so I could have my daily swig. I read somewhere that if you give your booze a different name it don't sound so bad. I'm know I'm not a drunk like Stella said. I could quit anytime I wanted, but that's the trouble, I don't want to. My life's only seems good enough when I'm half smashed.*

Yanking at the plastic cream-colored hand size remote that turns the TV on, controls the sound, and summons help; Hoochie repeatedly punched the button until an angry grayed haired nurse answered. "What is it you need?" she asked.

Just give me a few shots and a beer, that would kill this pain. What the hell are you here for?"

Betty Jean Giffell, the nurse had worked in this hospital for twenty years and had seen many an alcoholic suffer the pains of withdrawal. She knew that as soon as he slept for a while he would be ready to accept the unhappy fact that he needed alcohol. He must either quit it or it would kill him.

Hoochie raved and cursed for an eternity or so it seemed. When he finally fell into a fitful sleep, the rest of the 2nd. Floor breathed a sigh of relief.

"Pray he sleeps till morning," Nurse Jones said as she counted out the meds into a small paper cup, gave them to the little gray man lying quietly in the bed. Henry was in the next room to Hoochie, and Henry was fighting lung cancer. He had just finished a chemotherapy treatment and as is typical with most chemotherapy patients he was freezing cold, and tired beyond words.

An exhausted Henry simply nodded his head, bald from the chemotherapy treatments. His tired, lined face stretched into a grimace of a smile as Nurse Jones left the room.

Too bad that patient in the next room isn't as brave as Henry, Nurse Betty Jean thought as she peeked back into Henry's room, made the sign of the cross, then continued her rounds.

"I ain't been in a hospital since the old lady shit out that last kid and it ain't changed a bit." T.J groused. Tossing and turning his upper body Hoochie tried to find a position where the throbbing legs wouldn't hurt as much. He only accomplished the opposite reaction to his misery, bringing on more pain to his pounding legs. They all think they're all so dammed high and mighty but I bet they're hell on wheels when they ain't working.

Maybe if I holler loud enough they'll give me something to drink to kill this pain.

Nurse Betty Jean Giffell relaxed in the nurses lounge drinking coffee and thanking God she was here working instead of sitting at home with her aged mother.

Mrs. Gladys Giffell had suffered a slight stroke some ten years ago. Her left leg was a little difficult to manage but otherwise she was in good health. The stroke and its slight damage was just the extra leverage that Gladys Giffell needed to continue taking advantage of her unmarried daughter.

Nurse Betty Jean was aware of her mother's devious ways but had long ago abandoned her dream of a husband and children. Her hopes had been crushed when she caught her sister Ella in bed with her long time lover, David. He had never spoken of marriage, but after dating for six years Betty Jean naturally assumed that they would wed. Ella had moved out of the family home that very same day that she and David were caught. David moved into the small apartment with Ella the following week.

Betty Jean was devastated by the

betrayal of her sister and David, but Mrs. Giffell was secretly glad as she now had Betty Jean all to herself. It wasn't as though Mrs. Giffell didn't want what was best for her oldest daughter, it was just that as a loving parent she just wanted Betty Jean to find the right man. He had to be much better looking and more unintelligent than that slouch David, after all it was an honor for any man to be the father of Gladys Giffell's grandchildren.

    This is my refuge, Betty Jean thought as she checked the locked meds closet. Damn!! More Codeine's missing, must have missed counted, better check it again. Sure she had slipped David a little Codeine when his back was bothering him, but she hadn't given him any more since he ran off with with Ella. His dammed back wasn't bothering him when he was banging her sister.

    Mother always said he was a moocher and I guess she was right, but damn he sure was good in the sack. Mother is always pushing me toward Dr. Frank Swan, I wonder what she would say if she knew he and Dr. Steven James have been lovers for years. Maybe some day when she pushes me too far I'll drop that little bombshell.

Finding the missing drugs in behind the syringes, she breathed a sigh of relief. Going back to Henry's bedside, she held the glass of ice so he could taste the water that he couldn't swallow.

His eyes were filled with the gratitude that his mouth couldn't express. Henry reached out and touched Betty Jean's hand, the heat of his fever raced up her arm and touched her heart. Tears began to form and she knew she must get away before Henry seen them. Patting his hand gently, she turned and left the room. Her tears came welling out as she made her way to the bathroom, she needed time to think and pray, and It was time to change her sanitary napkin.

Meanwhile, back in Hoochie's room the T.V. Blared through out the whole floor and hall, the races were on and he'd be dammed if he'd miss them. Joan, the gal at the nurse's station had buzzed him, warning him, if he didn't lower the sound she would unplug his set, but he just yelled back, "Screw you."

"Well screw you too," Joan mumbled as she hit the switch that provided energy to Hoochie's T.V. Set.

Hoochie shouted into the intercom, "Hey,

my set ain't working, get the T.V. guy in here to fix it." There was no answer.

"Get your ass in here to fix or I'll fix it myself."

Still no answer.

Hoochie pulled himself up by the bed rail and tried to leverage his legs over the side of the bed. He felt his body tipping but didn't have the strength to stop himself from falling,That is when the waves of nausea began. The heat from the damaged legs tore over his whole body. Oblivion came in a rush and his twisted legs were trapped beneath his unconscious body.

Joan heard the crash and slowly walked to Hoochie's room, glancing at the man lying on the floor, her mind said, *this is the first peace and quiet we have had since he came in. I should leave him there for a while.* Dedication won over temptation, she rang for help to put him back in bed. One of the aids came running and helped put the unconscious man back into bed.

"I guess I had better notify the doctor about his little fall," Joan whispered to the aid, "but then again the doctors haven't had a break this whole night, best let them rest for a while, he sure as hell isn't going anyplace."

"You got that right," the mannish appearing nurses aid muttered while she was roughly shoving Hoochie's bent legs under the covers. "Does my heart good to see a bastard like him get his just deserts. My little sister married an asshole just like him. He ended up killing her."

Angela White left the hospital after watching the doctors treat a tiny beaten child whose papa had lost his temper according to the child. Heart heavy with grief she made her way to the drug store and had her heart medicine prescription refilled for the third time. Hands shaking she apologized to the druggist for dropping and breaking the last bottle he had filled for her. She had explained to the over worked pharmacist that She'd had a long day and even longer night trying to keep an abused wife from returning to her abuser. The women had a broken jaw, broken arm, and multiple bruises and how The women had refused to stay in the hospital, saying that if she stayed the police would get a report and arrest her husband.

Angela White tried to explain to the battered women that the police would get a report anyway as she had been treated in the emergency room, but the frightened victim would not lodge a complaint. The fear of another beating or the anguish over another threat of death for her and the children kept her frozen.

    The pharmacist, tired from a twelve hour day simply nodded and handed Angela her prescription and moved to the back of cubicle to pop another pick me up.

    Houchie woke with the worst pain in his life, his legs felt as though they were being ripped from his hips and the drugs that he needed to kill the pain still could not given to him or at least that is what that bitch of a nurse said when she peeked in to check on him. Staring at the stark white walls Hoochie seen the first bug come crawling out of the crack in the corner of the room.

    What the hell, this place is supposed to be clean and sanitary not have critters crawling around. First one, creature, then two, then they poured into the room like a flood of wiggling, snapping, creeping creatures filled with hate and memories, ready to drowned their victim. Closer and closer they came twisting and turning each one trying to get to

Hoochie first. They crawled up his legs, headed for his eyes, ears, and mouth. Every opening became an entry into the twisting, turning, bed ridden Hoochie and kept him from screaming. If he opened his mouth to scream they would get in and he would drown from the flow of the bugs into his throat.

This is the scene that Angela White saw as she gently pushed open the half closed door.

"Mr Miller, I don't know if you remember me. I'm the one who accidentally hit you and I am here to see if there is anything I can do to help."

To terrified to open his mouth to answer, Hoochie, eyes wide with fear, motioned toward the door and the nurse's station. *God dammit I need that stupid nurse right now, she can get these bugs off me before they eat me alive. What a fucked up way to die!*

Angela, not understanding what he was trying to say, left the room and shuffled down the empty hall. I didn't do this on purpose, she thought, but I feel so guilty. Things happen in life that bring us together with others and we have no control over the outcome. I just know this is one of these times. God will tell me what to do when the time comes. God has instructed me all these years and He won't let me down now.

"Hi Angela," nurse Betty Jean greeted the forlorn angel of mercy. *She is a saint,* thought the stressed out nurse Betty Jean. *She has helped so often when the patent has lost all hope. Most times she is there when they go to meet their maker, but she has given them the hope of a better life in the hereafter.*

Doctor Swan, having finished operating on the gunshot victim, came out to the nurse's station, checked Hoochie's chart and issued a mild sedative to relax him until they could administer a more potent drug for pain.

"Doctor, I believe the patient is going through the DTS and we are having difficulty restraining him"

"Tie him down, we don't have time for his shit." A very tired Doctor Frank Swan headed toward the stairs, leaving an exhausted nurse to deal with Hoochie. "When he cools down we can hit him with some drugs to keep him under control." Doctor Swan tossed these words over his shoulder, "I'm gong home, call me if you need me."

It had been days since Frank had seen Steven St.James and he was hungry for his loving touch. Just being held by him in tucked away closets and bathrooms was not enough, he needed more. Lighting another cigarette, he ignored the dirty looks he got from the security guard as he pushed his way out of the ambulance entrance. *Screw him, I earned this butt and I'm going to enjoy every drag.*

Dennis, had worked security here at this hospital for almost ten years and had seen many doctors come and go, to him they only thought they were gods. He knew better. *They think I don't see them sneaking around in the halls at night. I don't care if they diddle themselves to death, just so they don't act like their better then me. That asshole knows he ain't supposed to be smoking on hospital grounds.*

Frank dreaded going home to Franny, she was a sweet girl but she was not his love of choice. In the beginning he had worked so hard to prove that there was nothing wrong with him. He chased every skirt that he came in contact with, every twat that would spread her legs, just hoping that he could sort out these feelings of being incomplete. When Franny ended up pregnant he decided to do the honorable thing and marry her. Being married seemed like the answer at the time. The day he started his internship at Johns Memorial Hospital in South Dakota, he met Doctor Steven St. James. It was love at first sight. Steven with his dark curly hair and gorgeous blue eyes took Frank's breath away. The years Frank spent at Johns Memorial were the best years of his life. When Steven told him that he was accepting an offer from a small hospital in northern Michigan, Frank was devastated. His own true love moving away to god knows where leaving him to face the empty days without Steven.

"You could go with me," invited Steven. "There aren't that many interns applying to a small hospital for the kind of pay that you would be getting, but you're almost done with your internship and then the future could be brighter for both of us."

Frank applied and was accepted within the month. Franny didn't want to move to Hicksville, but if she wanted to stay with him she would go along or else.

The kid was the only thing holding him in this marriage and she knew it. Frank had even threatened to have a paternity test run on the kid and that cooled her down. Frank didn't give a shit if the kid was his or not, the little wife and kid were good cover.

Angela suspected that the two doctors had a secret and she could guess what that was, but that was not her concern. She only worried when one party was a victim. She could see no victims in this situation. She knew that Frank's wife was seeing one of the new interns on the sly and seemed perfectly content with the way her life was going. The kid was well taken care of and Frank sure didn't care if Franny cheated.

Making her way back to Hoochie's room she braced herself for the tyrannical outburst she knew was coming. Pushing open the door she peeked into the semi-dark room and was shocked to see the man in the bed cringing in terror.

What would make this macho man cower in the bed shaking like a leaf in a wind storm? She'd seen DTS before but this was the worst case she had ever seen, the only thing that he wasn't doing was the agonizing screaming that usually comes with these tremors. She wondered if any one had contacted his wife to tell her of his accident. Angela knew he had a wife because the nurse had complained that he continuously cursed that poor women for leaving him. Probably the best thing she could have done, taken the children out of that house before someone got hurt. I'll try and talk to him and see if he wants to contact his wife it's the least that I can do.

"Good morning Mr. Miller, do you remember me? My name is Angels White and I would like to help you in any way I can. Has anyone contacted your wife to let her know about your accident? I can see you're are in great pain and I will do anything I can do to help."

"Bring me a couple beers, that's what you can do," Hoochie mumbled.

What could have damaged this poor soul so badly that he can't face life without a drug? Angela asked herself. *I have met a few like him before and there is always some incident that is the sign post. My first opinion was premature, I'm sure he is a lost soul looking for someone who can live up to his expectations. God was right in choosing me. I'm willing to devote my life to helping God rectify the situation. A few chaff slip through during the separation of the wheat from chaff. Is Mr. Miller wheat or chaff, that is my job to find out. My gift is to help him solve the mystery before he ruins his life and I must save that precious family of his from destruction.*

Smiling her most angelic smile, Angela glided toward Hoochie with hand outstretched, her eyes were filled with unshed tears. She was always at her best when her patient's needs were uppermost in her undertakings for God. The Father in heaven always made the final decision as to if the patient lived or died and Mr. Miller was no exception.

Her touch sent shivers up and down his spine.
Was she was holding a needle that was filled with the drug he so desperately needed to end this pain? She had the most angelic smile Hoochie had ever seen, why couldn't all women be this way, he asked himself as the pain went and rapture seeped in. This is the way life should be all the time then I wouldn't have to drink to survive.

These were Hoochie's last thoughts.

Stella stood over the body of her husband trying to be brave in front of the attendant who was holding up the sheet so that she could see Hoochie's face.

"Yes, thats him. That's my husband T.J. Did the Doctor say what he died from?"

"You'll have to talk to Doc about that, but I'm guessing the booze had a lot to do with it," he answered. "You done looking yet? I got a lot of work to do and not much time until quiting time."

"Yes, I'm done, It is just a shock to me. The last I heard he just had a broken leg. In this day and age nobody dies from a broken leg do they?"

Anglia left the hospital and made her way back to her cozy little apartment satisfied that God had answered her once again. Of the many friends she had helped over the years, God had only seen fit to rescue two lives. It had always been God's decision, if they lived or died, she was only the instrument which He used to accomplish His will.

Anglia poured a saucer of milk for the small gray kitten that she had rescued from that dark filthy alley near the hospital, named him cuddles and held him while he drank the life giving liquid. The love birds in the purple cage watched as she fed the cat, cooed to each other and waited their turn for Anglia's attention.

"God has blessed me with this mission of mercy," she told the the contented stray kitten who was now lying in her lap permitting her to sooth him. The birds waited patiently, small black eyes watching every move she made. They knew the kitten wouldn't be there for very long, there had been other cats come into this household, some old, some young but they always disappeared after a while. Anglia couldn't abide the stalking nature of the cats she brought home, she always hoped that this one would be different, but they never were. When God told her to save them from their sinful ways she had to obey. Her heart would break each time she held them in the pail of water until the fighting stopped. She would miss them, but there would be others who would have the chance to beat the devil at his own game. Her work was never done.

Placing the kitten in her favorite chair, she fed the birds, heated a TV dinner for herself and thought about all the work she had on her schedule for tomorrow. Visit the nursing home where Mrs. Franklin waited for her to come and play cards. Mrs. Franklin cheated when playing every game, but Anglia didn't really care. Mrs. Franklin's cheating is what made Anglia decided to make tomorrow the cheater's last day. Cheating is a sin and she must save Mrs. Franklin from her evil self, then there is the old man who lives on third street, he don't really have a home, he lives in a box near the heat vent from Knudson's Cleaners, God told her that he had suffered enough, it was time he came home to his loving father. A good hot cup of coffee with just a little rat poison should do the job. He will be so much happier when he is saved from that wasted life.

    I'm sure God has placed others on this earth to help in saving his unrepentant sinners from themselves, maybe some day we can get together, but not right away, we still have much work to do and not enough days in the week.

The End

We've all know some one like Hoochie, we love him we hate him , we tolerate his foolishness, we walk away from his anger, but no matter what we do we are affected by his bad decisions.

B.N.

A Child Called Orange

    Even though her face was racked with the pain of withdrawal; and the drugs had taken their toll, she was still beautiful. Her wasted, pock marked arms reaching, eyes pleading for the needle that was filled with sweet relief. Her once attractive body was torn by the ravages of too many nights with the needle. The escape it offered was only temporary, but she needed it to live. Tomorrow would be her nineteenth birthday, "Happy frigging birthday,"she whispered.

    Two men were hunched over the painted table, scared from too many cigarettes burning out on the surface. Both were busy carefully measuring and packaging the white dust that lay in a small pile in the center of the table. They paid no attention to the now moaning women who was lying on the dirty mattress in the dingy, cold apartment.

    The girl's thoughts went back to the days when she still had hopes for the good life. She had salvaged this bed frame when she first came to the city. That long ago time when her mind was overflowing with plans for her future as a model. She had been so full of plans then, a lovely apartment, a wonderful job, and the kind of life that the beautiful people lived.

    The bright orange paint for the frame had been easy to find, but the soft green spread was a lot harder to locate. Then by chance she had seen the spread in the Penny's Catalog, just the right shade and on sale too. Her funds were getting low, but she had reasoned, this was the perfect spread and it would give her the lift she needed to face another long day of walking from one job prospect to another.

    Her mornings had been spent responding to ads in the newspaper, her evenings she had spent painting, hanging new wallpaper, anything to brighten up the dreary rooms she now called home.

    Her mind had raced a mile a minute, First, she had planned, I must find work, then I can afford to buy a couple of new outfits for my interviews with the modeling agencies. The apartment is cheap, and close enough to everything so I will save money getting to and from auditions.

On the day her cozy little nest was finished, she danced around the two tiny rooms, shaking her narrow hips and singing a song of joy. "I got it made, I'm going places, my lucky star is shinning down on me, I'm gonna make a new beginning, I got a plan, I just can't lose, I'm gonna be rich, rich, rich."

This path way to hell had its beginning on her fourteenth birthday. Edna Sue Hawkins was the youngest of six children and the last one still living at home. Her older siblings had gotten out as soon as they were old enough. Her sister Sandy was the last one to leave, two years ago. She had promised Edna Sue that she would come back for her, but she never did. After Sandy left, Papa started making his awful nightly visits to her room. Now Edna Sue knew why Sandy got out at the age of fifteen.

When Sandy didn't come for her in that first year Edna Sue lost hope of being rescued. She knew she must make plans to save herself.

Working at whatever jobs that were offered, she had saved every cent toward the time she could escape her bondage. She knew it was the only way she could survive. She had to make a new life like her brothers and sisters had.

When Edna Sue's mama had stashed away what she felt was a small fortune, she had taken her daughter aside and whispered, "You work so hard, I'm gonna buy you a pretty new dress. one that will fit you now that you are almost growed." When her father left for work, Mama finished cleaning the kitchen where Papa always flicked his ashes, he said it gave his old women something to do to keep her out of trouble.

Mother and daughter had grabbed their sweaters and gone out into the brisk, windy sunshine; excited about shopping for that special dress. At the local second hand store, they had browsed the racks until they worked their way to the dress section.

She remembered what she had told her mother that day, "Some day I'm gonna have a new-store bought dress and ain't I gonna be proud," It was as though she were living those days over again.

    Edna Sue remembered how she had felt as her fingers roamed through the dresses hanging on the rack. First she had checked colors. Her mind was racing, it ain't everyday a girl gets to buy a new dress, well, almost new. Red, that's it, I'll choose red. Now that's a purty red, but it's an old women's dress all long and ugly, purty color though. Here's a green one, but momma says I don't look good in green. It makes me all pastey. Now here's a purty one, purple with frills on the front, better keep looking. Here it is! It ain't red, but the next thing to it. It's orange, and that's a special color. Not red, not yellow, but the two all mixed up together it comes out orange. This is the dress for me! Even Mama's smiling. Better try it on to make sure.

    She had taken her prize to the dressing room, pushed the curtain aside and hurriedly took off the faded rag she was wearing. As she slipped the silky garment over her head, her dark curly locks lovingly stroked the glorious fabric. It had clung to her as though caressing her, as the fine strands slipped down over the ragged undershirt, and white cotton panties, covering her near naked body.

She remembered hearing mama's voice hollering, "You come on out of there when your dressed, I wanna see how you look, and if it fits right. Can't be buying you a new dress every month, it's gotta last at least a year."

Better get out there and see what mama says. She's just gotta love it cause I just gotta have it. She had bent her head and said a silent prayer. Edna Sue was reliving that wonderful day as though she were still there.

Hesitantly emerging from the small, dusty room, she'd stood hugging the door frame, her heart pleading for approval.

"Hurry up, we ain't got all day, Mama had complained, 'Papa will be expecting supper on the table when he gits home. it'll be hell to pay if it ain't hot and ready when he gets in that door."

"Mama, this dress was made for me. It knows it, just like I know it. I can tell by the way it holds me." Edna Sue laughed as she remembered her excitement that day.

"Git all the way out here so's I can see you." Mama had shouted

She'd quickly hustled out to show mama the magic dress that was going to change her life forever.

Edna Sue had felt like a princess as she strolled into the small hallway that led to the changing room. Her feet had glided across the warped wooden floor, as though she was floating. Even the world seemed newer; the shabby room had glowed with a rosy hue.

Mama's still smiling, Edna Sue remembered saying, silently glorying in her good fortune, "Thank you God!"

The orange color had seemed too bright when it hung on its hanger, but now perfect on this lovely little girl, subdued, the tangerine shade complimented the dusky complexion of the child, her tousled black locks came alive against the vivid color of the dress. It was just large enough to suit mama, and just tight enough to please the girl.

"Oh, I wish I could wear this dress forever,"she had sung out, as she gracefully twirled for her mother. I feel like a princess, I never felt this good in my whole life."

A smiling mama had said yes, she could wear the dress home.

The ecstatic girl drew the stares of passersby, not just men, but women too, gazed at the vision of loveliness passing them on the filthy, garbage-strewn street.

A hobo staggering into a doorway, lowered his paper wrapped bottle of wine, long enough to tip his crumpled felt hat, sweep his arm out in an exaggerated courtly bow as he fell into his cubbyhole for the night. Perhaps dreaming of queens and princesses.

When the bubbly girl and her proud mother had arrived home, her father had taken one look and roared, "You look like a slut, git that thing off, and I don't want to see it again. Old women, you don't spend my hard earned money on glad rags for any daughter of mine." Grabbing a can of beer out of the scarred old refrigerator, he had turned on his frightened wife with a fury born of long days in a dirty foundry and too little pay. Needing a victim, he'd shouted, "What in the hell is wrong with yer head old women, ain't you got a brain in yer noggin? That girl's gonna have boys sniffing around here soon enough with out her advertising."

Edna Sue's mother had begun sobbing, "Yer right, but she looked so good, reminded me of my first growed up dress. I was so proud of how I looked, I felt like all the good things in the world was coming to me.

"I can't take it back, cause she wore it, but

I kin pack it away until she is old enough. Guess I forgot how young she is. She acts so growed up, what with all the baby setting, house cleaning jobs, and running errands, she jist seems so much older. I didn't really spend any money on that dress, she did. It was her money from working all those jobs."

    My mama lied, but was the first time that she had ever did anything to protect any of her children. She must have been getting soft in her old age.

    "Well, she shouldn't be spending her money on whore dresses," Papa had grumbled, "she should give the money to me to invest for her."

    The girl listened at the closed door of her room, "Damn him," she had mumbled, "I wish he was dead! Papa never invested in anything but all the booze he could drink, he did help keep the beer company in business. He just wants to keep me around for him and his damned sneaking around stuff. If I tell Mama she's gonna say its my imagination, he wouldn't do anything bad to me Her anger grew as she remembered the bad things he had done to her, his foul breath had seared her soul, and the the rejection she felt when

Mama ignored his touching her small breast and his saying, "small breast, small hole." Mama had pretended that it is all just kidding or a bad dream.

"Girl" papa had said, "get that whore dress off and git out here and help yer mama, next I suppose yer gonna want to paint yer face with all that shit called makeup." The smirking old man had gone back to sucking on his can of beer, and shaking his cigarette ash on the floor that his wife had scrubbed that very morning.

The dress went into the only decent piece of furniture in the whole house, Mama's hope chest. That's a laugh, thought the angry child, there ain't much hope for Mama anymore. I know she used to be pretty, cause I seen their wedding picture, before he tore it to shreds one night in a drunken rage. I remember him beating hell out of her, slamming her head against the wall and kicking her when she fell on the floor. If thats love, I'll pass! I'll marry for money; at least you get something out of it besides a dump to live in and a poke full of kids.

The year had gone ever so slowly for the girl; who had tried to save, and dreamed of the day she could leave there forever. Mama seemed to understand and share her yen to get away, but she had refused to see the obvious signs of sexual abuse. Edna Sue slept only when her father was too drunk to visit her room.

Once, she had tried to talk to her mother about the visits in the middle of the night; but her mother had covered her ears screaming, that she misunderstood her father's intentions toward her. She never tried again, but she had bought a lock for her bedroom door and installed it when he was at work. She lay and listened to his ranting and raving the first time he tried to enter after the lock was in place. Her heart had been pounding, and she was shaking, but he stopped making his nightly visits.

Mama began to change after that; it was as if she wanted her daughter to leave the house too, was she jealous of her own child or did she resent the fact that now she was the recipient of the drunken man's attacks of lust?

While talking to one of her school friends, Betsey, the details of her horrible situation had burst forth from Edna Sue's mouth. She could not stop the mountain of pain that had rolled from her shivering lips.

Edna Sue remembered Betsey sitting and listening in shocked silence. She could not absorb all that Edna Sue was telling her and her eyes widened in disbelief. At last she realized what danger her friend Edna Sue was in and she had whispered, "Tell a teacher, tell someone, anyone," Betsey had pleaded, "My God, you don't have to live that way!"

"I can't tell anybody," the frightened girl had explained, "they won't believe me, and Papa said he'll tell them I wanted it, and I came on to him. Every body at school will think I'm a slut.

"Well, they don't need to worry I will be out as soon as I kin. Dear God, just give me another year of his leaving me alone and a chance to save. I believe I can make it on my own."

If God was listening that day it was with a deaf ear. That very night her father had broken her bedroom door and took her with such force that even her mother tried to come to her aid. Kicking and screaming; her mother had attacked the father with a broom,swinging it full force, she had knocked the drunken fool unconscious. "Run," she told the girl, "git all yer things and run for dear life."

That is exactly what Edna Sue did. Dashing through the house, she'd gone to her mother's battered old cedar chest, threw open the top, and there was her beautiful orange dress. It was just as she remembered it. Touching it was like meeting an old friend, one you hadn't seen for a while. She held it, and caressed it. In her heart she knew this was the right time to leave her father's house, and not look back. Hanging the dress over her arm; she had run to the bathroom, slipped the money she had saved, out of its hiding place under the toilet, and left the house before he woke up.

All hell would break loose when he woke up. Poor Mama, now was her time to leave, but she probably wouldn't. He could almost kill her and she wouldn't leave.

The money Edna Sue had saved was tucked into her bra, she felt the folded bills scratching her breast. It had given her great comfort to know that for a change, a good thing was causing the hurt.

Edna Sue had trudged to the bus station,

asked the clerk for a ticket on the very next bus leaving town.

The man behind the counter hadn't wanted to sell her a ticket. He told her she was too young to be going out on her own. He, smiled with a lecherous leer, called her sweetie, then suggested that she needed an adult to look after her.

Edna Sue, giving one of her most charming smiles, had lied and told him she was eighteen and could travel anywhere she pleased.

He had reached out and patted her hand and said,"Well; alright little lady, but if you change your mind, I get out at midnight. We could have something to drink and get to know each other better. I could be awfully friendly to a sweet little girl like you."

She remembered thinking, *are all men pigs or is there something wrong with me? Do I do something that makes them act that way?* She had taken the ticket, and walked to the far end of the station. Choosing a seat away from the others who were waiting for their buses, she sat down and began to dream, just a little.

No one had paid any attention to the girl

with an orange dress hung over her arm and a paper sack on the bench beside her.

Chicago, that's were the clerk said she was going. She had heard that they hired models in Chicago too, not like New York of course, but she didn't have enough money for a ticket there anyway, so the windy city it is.

This is the part of the story where she completely loses herself in the past. It is as though she went back to that crucial point in her life, reliving her past like an old time movie.

The bus pulled along side the terminal; shinning lights into the waiting room, startling the half dozing girl. Jumping up she started for the door, then she remembered the sack with her few meager belongs crammed into it, she turned and ran back, just as an old women was picking it up. Edna Sue reached out for the sack, but the old women pulled it closer to her chest, saying, "This here is my sack and you can't have it!"

Edna Sue couldn't believe her ears, this women was lying, and there was nothing she could do about it. She looked around for someone to come to her aid, but none were looking her way. "Please," she pleaded, " it's just my clothes. They won't fit you, and I really need them."

The clerk was watching from the window, but he didn't make a move to help. The old women caught sight of the clerk staring at her; she snickered and asked the girl, "How much will you give me for this bag?"

"All I have left is a dollar. My ticket took all the rest." It was a lie, but thats all she had in her pocket, and she'd be dammed if she would let the old women see she had more. Beside it wasn't fair that she had to pay to get her own clothes back!

The old women reached for the money with her right hand and held out the sack with her left, but Edna Sue was too quick for her. She grabbed the bag; and ran like hell, still holding the dollar, she jumped on the bus, took a seat, and stared out the window. The angry old women was shaking her fist and shouting at her through the glass. Edna Sue stuck her tongue out just as the bus was pulling away. The gesture infuriated the old women, who was left holding empty air for all her effort.

I gotta stay on my guard with strangers, I guess I can't trust anybody, just like Timbo said. He would have ran away with me, if he wasn't in jail. The worst part is, he didn't do this crime, Frankie did it, but Timbo was in the wrong place, at the wrong time. Oh well, if he was innocent this time, next time he won't be, so it all evens out, she'd told herself,

    Edna Sue remembered flattening out the sack as best she could, slid it under her bottom, covered her legs with the orange dress, snuggled down into the seat, and promptly fell asleep. When she woke, the bus was pulling into the station outside the city of Gary, Indiana. The driver told the passengers that they would have a fifteen minute layover, then on to Chicago. The excitement began to build for the girl; her dreams were starting to come true. She got off the bus; used the facilities, washed her hands, splashed her face, and brushed her hair, then went back and sat in the same seat she had before. An ice cold feeling invaded her whole being. My bag is gone! Damn it the freaking bag is gone. Why in hell did I leave the bus to pee, I could have held it a while longer. She raged in her mind, while her eyes frantically searched the passengers and their seats on the bus.

    Catching sight of a handsome young man

coming toward her and in his arms he was carry her sack. She nearly fainted. What in hell does he want for my bag? I ain't giving him any money for it! He can stick it you know where before I'll give him a dammed dime. I don't care how good looking he is, I'm not going to fall for his crap.

Flashing Edna Sue a wide, beautiful smile, he had handed her the sack. He sat down in the seat facing her and explained, "I seen the trouble you had at the last station, when the old women grabbed your bag. I didn't want it to happen again. You have to be careful of who you trust, where ever you are."

"I know," she had agreed, "but I just keep forgetting about that stupid bag. I guess I'm just too trusting."

'Well, he had said, "you're lucky you ran into me, I can help you get settled when we get to Chi Town. I know a lot of people, and I do have a little influence. We will have see that you find work when we get there."

Sure you will, she thought, *right out of the goodness of your heart. Well this gal ain't gonna believe anything you say. You're much too pretty to have to pick up strays at bus stations. Besides I don't trust anyone prettier* than me. You got something up your sleeve.* She had smiled at him, pretending she believed every word he said, after all she was street smart, a gal had to be to survive. If she said it often enough maybe she would come to believe it.

Tommy knew the signs, he had seen them hundreds of times. *These stupid cunts came to the big city from some little Podunk, where they were queen of the may. They come here thinking the whole town is waiting just for them. When they don't become famous in a month they're ready to do anything to survive.* Well bitch, I got news for you, I can be real patient, it won't take long and then you're mine. He smiled back at the unworldly girl sitting across from him. *She will make a welcome addition to his harem, a sweet young piece like her.*

When they arrived at the main terminal, she had grabbed her twice rescued sack and dashed for the ladies room. Once inside she put a coin in the slot, entered the stall, and relieved herself. Going to the soaped stained wash basin, she washed her face, brushed her hair and prayed that the man from the bus was gone. Peeking out the door and seeing no one she knew, she picked up her precious bag and headed for the EL station. On the platform she puzzled over which way to go to find a place that had cheap rent and was close to model agencies. Taking a paper from the rack by the door, she leafed through the want ads. Most of the rooms with cheap rent were on the north side, so, she decided that was the way to go. Putting the neatly folded paper back in the rack she made her way to the closest station and waited.

Catching the North Carpenter St. train, she sat on the edge of the seat, afraid she would pass her destination and not know it. Glancing around the half filled train, she spotted the man from the bus. He raised his hand in salute, smiled, and turned to look out the window at the scenery whizzing by.

Well, what do you know, he's not mad at me for giving him the slip at the bus station. Maybe he's not so bad after all. Edna Sue pulled her sack closer, hugged it to her breast and day dreamed about a place of her own. A bright, cheery place, not like the apartment her mom and dad lived in. She could almost smell the odor of rancid grease that overpowered you when you walked through the door. Mama fried everything, that's the way papa liked it, the greaser the better. My place will never smell that way, she silently vowed.

South Jefferson was coming up, the train stopped and she got off. Feeling scared and very, very small, she questioned her decision to leave home. At least there she knew what to expect. *No,* she thought, *I have to be on my own and prove to the world that I'm a person. Besides I can't take another day of Daddy's mauling!*

The news paper says there is a room for rent on South Canal. I wonder how far that is.

After walking for blocks she finally saw the sign that read South Canal Street. My God, I thought I 'd never get here, now if I can find the right house, all the numbers here are funny, not like home. Lets see if I can figure it out. 1010 1/2 is here so 1011 must be here, but it isn't. Where in hell is it? Wait, there it is across the street, now how did they come up with that?

Softly knocking on the door of 1100 she waited. No answer. She pounded harder, still no answer. Why would they put an ad in if there was no one to a answer the door?

Just as she was about to leave, the door flew open and a harried looking women shouted, "Didn't you hear me hollering that I was coming? Little girl, you gotta have a little patience."

"I'm sorry," she stuttered, I didn't hear you. Maybe I was pounding to hard to hear you answer."

"Naw," answered the women with frazzled hair and face to match, "I was out on the back stoop and it takes a lot to hear that far. Did you want to see the room or not?"

"Oh yes, I would like to see the room; but I need to know how much the rent is, and if I can afford it."

"Well kid, the rent is a hundred a month. Can you afford that? It ain't much to look at, but it's warm in winter and cool in summer. Are you alone, where do you work, and how often do you have company?" The women continued the questions as she led the girl up through the dark dingy hallway to the ugliest room Edna Sue had ever seen. Every thing was brown, brown walls, brown drapes, brown bed spread hung crazily over a brown wooden bed.

"If I take it," the reluctant renter asked,

"would you mind if I changed a few things?"

"Honey, you pay the rent and you can do anything you want, as long as it's in good taste."

Edna Sue almost lost her composure when she heard that. What did the landlady call good taste, this horrid, dark room? She bit her tongue and smiled, it took every ounce of willpower for her to not burst out laughing. She counted out a pile of fives and tens until she had enough for two months rent. She told the cranky old women, that she would be moving in right now. Holding up the paper sack, she told the women this was all her luggage, she liked to travel light.

The women furrowed her brow and stared at Edna Sue, "Are you old enough to be out on your own?"

"Oh definitely," the frightened girl answered, "I just look young for my age. Everyone tells me that!"

The women shrugged her shoulders and muttered, "No skin off my ass if you ain't, I did my part, I asked. " The old women was recounting the pile of cash, as she made her way down the stairs.

Thank God she isn't one of those do-gooders, I could be on my way back home by now, if she was.

The so called room was actually two rooms with an arch separating them The smallest room held a hot plate, a battered old refrigerator, a small wooden table, and a white metal cupboard hanging from the wall above the sink. One rickety chair leaned against the ugly papered wall. The large apples in the wall paper had turned brown with age and heat, reminding the girl of the rotted fruit she had seen in the back of Mr. Henry's store back home. The larger room held the bed and a chest of drawers; both were the same ugly brown coloring that dominated the whole place.

"Ugh," she flinched as she surveyed the dark ugly room. "Just gotta do something about this mess first." Pulling open the top drawer of the chest she spotted an old newspaper dotted with mouse droppings. "Oh shit, now I gotta mouse to deal with," Edna Sue grumbled as she went to the top of the stairs to inform the landlady about the uninvited guests. Then she remembered that she hadn't gotten the women's name. She decided, since she couldn't holler, hey you, to the landlady, she would have to go down and find her.

Going down the filthy, litter filled stairs, she debated if she should shout or go into the womens part of the house. When she reached the bottom, she had decided to do both. Walking slowly, she began to shout, "Hello, hello, is anybody here?"

"You know dammed well I'm here,"came the answer, "I just left you! What do you want now?"

Edna Sue stammered, "I just wanted to let you know that the room has mice, I was just wondering if you had any rat poison"

"Honey, thats your room now, if you have mice, thats your problem. I rented the room as is. Honey you can call me Mrs, Touhy, but don't call too often! " The women laughed hilariously at her own nauseous sense of humor.

A sick feeling began in the girl's stomach. Screwed again! Into her mind popped a million questions. What is wrong with these people, is everyone in Chicago as cold hearted as this women? Doesn't anybody have sympathy for a newcomer, and why in hell am I here? Then she remembered what she had left behind. She knew she could learn to live with anything, except the hell she had back there.

Edna Sue turned, face burning from humiliation, and stomped back up the stairs, kicking garbage as she went. In her depressing room she threw herself on the rumpled bed. Shaking with anger, she vowed to make that women sorry she had treated a desperate girl so badly.

When she had calmed down enough to feel the demanding pangs of hunger, food was what she needed. Making sure that her money was tucked into her bra, she pinned it to the strap, left her sack on the bed, locked the door, and made her way to the street.

It looked as though the entire neighborhood women were sitting on their stoops, or hanging out windows, trying to catch the slight breeze that fought its way through the tall buildings and narrow streets. Children were playing ball in the street, dodging in and out of traffic, when they went for the ball.

Edna Sue remembered feeling a pang of jealously; those kids were about her age and they were playing as though they didn't have a care in the world. For her those days were gone forever.

Walking fast by the shouting children, her eyes had searched for some where to find food, anything that would ease the hunger in her growling stomach. She spotted a pizza place on the next block. It looked clean and there were a few families eating at small round tables. She opened the door, went inside and was greeted by a man wearing a white tee shirt, tan pants and a soiled white apron wrapped around his rotund body. A white chef's hat sat at right angles on his gray head. A smiling face completed the picture.

I wonder what he wants, she thought, people don't smile like that for nothing.

"Can I help you little lady?" the man asked, "We got some nice fresh crust and fixings. I can make you a delicious pizza in just a shake of a lambs tail."

"Yes sir," replied Edna Sue, "you can fix me a small one with pepperoni and mushrooms."

As the man began to knead and twirl the dough he continued to talk to Edna Sue.

She knew the man was trying to be friendly but instinct took over and she pretended that she hadn't heard him.

"You must be new to the neighborhood, I haven't seen you around here before and I'm sure I would remember."

"Yes , we just moved in, and no you haven't seen me around."

"Welcome to the neighborhood," said Sammy Schultz, the owner of this small shop in the center of this big city.

We're a pretty close knit bunch of neighbors, you know, kinda take care of each other. I've here all my life, you wanta know anything just ask me."

"Thanks I will. Is my pizza done yet? I'm starving!"

"Yes mam, it sure is ready and you never tasted a better pizza in your young life! Better be careful its hot."

Edna Sue had taken the steaming pizza to a small table in the front of the shop; sat down facing the glass window and began to eat the first real food she'd eaten since coming to the big city.

Sammy carried over a large glass full of ice water, set it in front of the girl, then went back behind the counter.

When the pizza was half gone, Edna Sue

remembered wondering how she was going to get the rest home to her apartment with out getting it all over her dress. I should have asked for it to go, but I didn't want to eat my first meal in that filthy place I have to call home. The girl sadly shook her head and stared at the man behind the counter. Now I gotta go beg for a box to carry it in.

 Sammy seeing her obvious distress, walked over to the table and handed her a Styrofoam container.

 When she asked him how much he just waved his hand and smiled again.

 I can't believe this, he's too good to be true, gotta watch my step with this guy. Edna Sue hurriedly put the pizza in the box and pushed open the door. She heard Sammy say, "Come back again soon," but she didn't answer.

 As she passed an old dilapidated apartment house further down the block, she spied an old metal bedstead lying propped against the overflowing garbage cans that lined the street. Its paint was yellowed and scared from years of neglect, the metal scroll work begged for attention from a caring owner. The forlorn bedstead seemed to call to the girl, saying, See me, I'm just what you need. I will hold you and give you rest.

She knew she was being foolish but she just had to have that bed. Now, she thought, I just have to figure out how to get that heavy old frame up to my place. She sat down on a cement porch nearest where the bedstead was piled and reasoned, which is more important, my breakfast or the bed.

The bed won. Edna Sue knew if she ran home to put the leftover pizza in the refrigerator, the bed would be gone when she got back. "Well," she said, "here goes nothing, setting the Styrofoam box on the highest step. She dug out the heavy side bars that were buried in trash; pulled them to where the head and foot boards were, she then tied them all together with an old piece of rope that was lying in the junk When she lifted her heavy burden she knew that she would have to slide it most of the way home. She pulled an old rug from the garbage heap and placed it under the part of the frame that would be dragging on the ground. She began to pull the prized bedstead down the dim street.

Looking back at the porch where she had left her pizza, she saw a stray dog sniffing the box, preparing to have tomorrows breakfast as his mid-day snack. With sweat dripping down her face and arm pits, she knew she would rather have this symbol of her freedom. Thats okay mutt, you only have the pizza, I have the bed, She gloated.

Folks sitting on their porches hoping to catch the last frail breeze before they had to retreat to their hot stuffy apartments, watched as Edna Sue dragged her heavy load toward the house at the end of the block. None offered to help, some even made bets on her progress. As she passed, they snickered at her determination. One old fellow crudely remarked, "Honey I got a bed for ya."

After what seemed like ages, she reached her destination.

The landlady saw her hauling the heavy frame to the stairs and commented, "Thats quite a load you have there little girl, pretty heavy for you to haul all alone. Just don't go skinning up my woodwork!" She continued on her way to the back of the house.

"Thanks for all your help," Edna Sue mumbled under her breath. Exhausted she pulled the prize up the stairs one at a time. When she finally got to to the top, she carefully leaned her burden against the wall while she unlocked and opened the door. Pulling the bed frame in with her very last ounce of strength she flicked on the light to her apartment. Her wonderful find looked even worse under the bright glare of the hanging light. That will be my next project, she thought as she looked at the bare bulb hanging down on a dirty brown cord from the cracked ceiling "That has to go," she had whispered to the empty room.

    Edna Sue wished that she had enough energy to take the old ugly brown bed down right now but she didn't have any strength left. She decided to take a short nap before she tore down that ugly old thing that came with the apartment. Taking off her dress and hanging it on the one nail in the closet. Clad in only a too small underslip she laid down on the lumpy, stained mattress. As she was falling asleep, her mind was processing the information that the soil spots were probably piss stains, at least she hoped that was all it was.

    When she woke, her first thought was, did I remember to lock the door? Throwing herself off the bed and running to the old battered door, she turned the knob and it refused to open. "Yes, I did lock it, thank god for that!

She went to the kitchen area, poured water into a battered old pan and turned on one of the two burners of the greasy hot plate. "Yuck," she recalled whispering, "Everything in this place needs cleaning."

Here again she relived her first days in her new home as though she were there.

Going down the hall to the shared bathroom she found a pail that was bent and rusty but still serviceable. *How can people live this way? Our place was rundown but at least the things that came in contact with our bodies were clean. Mama saw to that.*

The first place she had to clean is where that ugly old brown bed stood. She wished she had someone to help move it out of her rooms, it was grimy from untold hundreds sleeping or what ever else they did, and that thought gave her chills.

"Oh shit, I need some cleaning soap or whatever they use to scrub off a hundred years filth. There goes more money and I don't even have a job yet, but I can't rest until I get this place cleaned up.

I gotta watch my mouth; ladies don't swear that way and especially models. Important people talk refined. I read that one in my romance magazines.

I better get myself to the store and get that damned soap, oops I did it again!"

She put her dress back on and went into the dirty streets of Chicago's north side.

The hardware in the middle of the tenth block was just closing as she came through the front door. The man was getting ready to lock up and told her she had five minutes to find what she needed. He wasn't gonna catch hell from his old lady for being late for supper.

She asked if he had any cleaning soap. He furrowed his forehead and thought for a minute, then answered, "If you mean cleaning products, yes we do, the last shelve in the corner. How the hell old are you anyway?"

Edna Sue pretended she didn't hear him, grabbing a bottle of Lysol she rushed to the counter to pay the man before he could ask any more questions.

"Kid are you new in the neighborhood? Where are your folks? Must be new letting you run loose in this hell hole. Ya need anything else?"

"You know, I am eighteen, old enough to be on my own, and no I don't need any thing else except a strong arm to help me clean my place."

"Where do you live and how much can you pay?" He asked.

"I can't pay anything," Edna Sue confided, "thats the trouble, if I could pay I wouldn't be stuck with the job."

"Wait while I see what my boy is doing, if he ain't busy I'll send him over to help," The man came back and told her that he couldn't find his son right now but he should be home soon.. "And as far as pay we can always work something out later."

The girl gave the man at the store her address and started for home. As she walked she mentally kick herself for trusting a complete stranger. "You damned fool," she berated herself, "now he knows where you live."

"Oh shit, here comes pretty boy from the bus," Edna Sue muttered, "well maybe he can help me get rid of the hardware man's son, then I'll worry about how to get rid of him.

"Hi little girl, how you doing in the big city? My dad says you need help with cleaning your place. I'm not busy at the moment so I could give you a hand. my name is Thomas, but all my friends call me Tommy"

"Thank God it's you, I thought I was dealing with someone I don't know. I was just kicking myself for giving out my address to a stranger. My name is Edna Sue, and I will be glad to have you help me"

"Well Edna Sue, you don't have to worry about me, I will help you no strings attached. I have a feeling we are going to be very good friends."

The two young people talked all the way back to Edna Sue's rooms. Tommy helped her move the heavy brown bedstead down to the basement, clean the floors and take down the heavy, dusty drapes.

She taped some newspaper over the now sparkling windows. The rooms took on a warm and homey feeling.

Tommy decided they should celebrate the new look with a bottle of wine. He assured Edna Sue that he wasn't a drinker either, but this was a special occasion. He convinced her that they should make it a day to remember.

While Tommy ran to the liquor store on the corner, Edna Sue washed her face and combed her hair, making herself presentable for the happy affair. What she really wanted was to be alone in her now cheery home, not drinking booze with a strange man. I can't be rude to him but I'll give him the bums rush after he has had his drink. I really do appreciate his help but I've got to be rested so I can go job hunting tomorrow and it looks like he's planning to stay late.

Tommy came bouncing in with a bottle of cheap wine, a package of cubed cheese and a box of crackers. Waving the cracker box, he shouted, "This is for our celebration, we earned this little snack."

When the girl woke the next day, Tommy was in the bed beside her. With aching head and rumbling stomach, she tried to remember what happened.

"Hey, your awake. Do you aways sleep that sound? I thought you were going to get up early and go job hunting"

"What happened," she asked, "Why are you still here?"

"Come on baby, don't you remember drinking most of the bottle and coming on to me? Not that I'm complaining. You're a good lay," Tommy added.

"I don't believe you! I've never done that before, why would I start now?"

"Honey, I don't know why, but I'm sure glad you did. Like I said before, we are going to be very good friends."

She inched out of the bed, grabbed a sheet to cover her naked body and ran to the kitchen area. Grabbing clothes from the broken chair, she peeked out into the hall. Seeing no one she stumbled to the bathroom down the hall.

When she had showered and dressed she returned to the room to find Tommy gone. "Thank you God! I won't ever let him touch me again." The wine bottle was still on the table reminding her of those lost hours spent with a stranger.

She peered into the mirror that hung from a nail over the cracked porcelain sink; stared at the tired looking face that stared back. "You look like hell," she told the girl in the mirror. "If thats how your gonna behave you could of stayed at home. Get your act together, ladies don't behave that way, jumping in the sack with every pretty boy she meets."

Edna Sue spent the rest of the day rearranging the place she now called home.

Tomorrow I will be rested and feeling a little better about myself, then I can go job hunting, she promised herself

In the morning, with the sun shining, the world looked like a better place to live. She went grocery shopping at the nearest market. I can't live on just pizza, I need a lot of vegetables in my diet. All the books said so. Why some models were even vegetarian's, the books said that too, but I don't think I can give up meat completely.

She dropped the food off at her new home and decided to spend the rest of this sunny day shopping. Picking up a gallon of salvage paint at the local Sears Store, she pretended she was just another famous model on her day off. Finding a small shop tucked in between two pawn shops, she wandered through looking at all the extras she would buy when she had a job.

Today is not the day to job hunt, her mind told her. She needed to rest and make a plan. I have too many things to sort out in my mind. Maybe tomorrow will be a better day to go searching for work. When morning came she still wasn't ready to face the world she had chosen for herself.

She spent the next few days cleaning and painting the bedstead, scrubbing walls, and hanging the lace curtains she had found at the Salvation Army Store.

When noon of the sixth day came she was feeling much better, her confidence had been restored by all the hard work that she had accomplished in such a shot time. The hell with it, she thought, I got to leave sometime and if I run into Bobby I 'll just ignore him. Starving, and wanting to get out in the sunshine, she bathed and put on her treasured orange dress. It had been so long since she had worn it that she had forgotten how familiar it felt to her skin. "I love this dress, it makes me feel so special!" she sang out as she stepped out of the dark, dingy hallway and into the sunbaked streets of Chicago.

The warm afternoon sun had enticed the apartment dwellers out to their stoops to enjoy the mild breezes that filtered down between the dilapidated buildings that lined the street.

They had stared at the young girl prancing jauntily down the street. The women of the rundown tenements, worn from too many hard days, and too many children, sat wishing they looked like this stunning girl. Their men were wishing it too!

The weather made the girl yearn for time to enjoy the many outdoor activities that were offered in Chicago. She would like to visit the zoo; go to Lake Michigan and watch the boats come and go, but there was no time for that right now, she must find work. I Can't make a living like that, she argued with temptation. Her money was going fast and no money coming in.

As she strolled along, she drew a lot of attention from the cars passing. They gawked and honked but she was so wrapped up in her dreams, she didn't realize that all the commotion was about her.

Edna Sue had wandered out of her familiar neighborhood into an even seamier part of the city. The garbage wasn't neatly stacked like it was on her block, instead it was piled in haphazard fashion on or near the curb. A pack of dogs were fighting over the cardboard containers and strewing the contents all over the sidewalk. She had to step carefully to avoid the stinking mess. Edna Sue's thoughts were on the wonderful new jobs that she was going to get. The many offers to model for big time magazines, the chance to travel and see other parts of the world.

She didn't notice the two swarthy men who were following close behind until it was too late. A huge hand went over her mouth, a sinewy leg wrapped itself around her legs and held her tight against his other leg. The attacker dragged her into a litter filled alley and began to tear at her dress.

Her eyes searched wildly for someone to help, but there was no one. Edna Sue knew that unless she used her head she was going to be raped and murdered here in this dank musty place and would never live out her dream. She made herself relax, she knew she had to play it smart if she wanted to survive. Edna Sue remembered the story she had read about another girl in this same situation. By using her wits the girl in the story had saved herself. She had pretended to be interested in the attacker until she saw a car coming. She had flung herself out into the street, away from the man who was trying to shove her into the back seat of his car. Edna Sue thought, maybe her story of courage will save me too.

Leaning into the captor and rubbing seductively she smiled up at the snaggle toothed man who was squeezing her breast until it felt as though it was being torn from her body. Edna Sue reached down and fondled his crotch, he spread his legs, releasing her legs and loosed his hold on her breast.

Edna Sue looked him straight in the eye, saying how good it was to find a man that ain't afraid to take what he wants. "I'm tired of dealing with these mama's boys who are worried about rubbers and such. Just because a girl's got a little ole touch of something don't mean she can't have a little nooky once in a while."

"You bitch!, what the hell you doing wiggling yer ass all over town if you got a dose. I don't want that shit, it burns."

"Oh, it ain't the clap, it's that virus thing that's going around. I forgot what the doc called it, hov, ive, or something like that. You don't get sick from it for along time, it ain't nothing to be scared of. I still need a little jump every now and then."

"Git the hell outa here, I ain't taking no chances with this dick of mine. It's the only one I got. Its sluts like you that spread that shit around."

The other man stood leaning against a tumbling down brick building, toothpick twisting rapidly in his sneering mouth, and an evil glint in his hungry eyes. "Hell." he whispered, "I already got a dose so it don't make no difference to me, might as well enjoy myself while I'm still here."

The shaking girl had reached down and grabbing the hem of her, pulled it up just enough to be seductive. "Come on honey, lets get it on before the cops get here." She prayed desperately that her prediction of cops coming would be true.

"What cops are ya talking about? The men sneered, they ain't never no cops dare come down here alone in daylight and don't never come after dark. We take care of our own problems in this neck of the woods. You must be new around here or you'd know that."

"Come on Frankie," urged the man who had been holding Edna Sue, "you don't want to mess with that shit, she don't look like she'd even be a good piece of ass."

"Ya, Davy, yer right."Frankie agreed, "I got me a dose but it ain't lasting, that hiv shit is hard stuff, they ain't got no cure for that. No piece of ass is worth that."

"Yer lucky, bitch, next time keep yer ass outta our neighborhood, this here is our turf, What we want we take, remember that! Now git the hell outta here before we mess you up real good."

Edna Sue ran blindly toward the first opening she saw and threw up at the entrance of the filthy alley. She frantically looked around; seeing a street light she ran to it and grabbing the post, laid her burning face against the tepid metal. The shivery fear crept through her flaming cheeks into her terrified mind and had lain like a chunk of ice in her pounding heart.

"What have I let myself in for, why did I come to this town anyway? These questions raced around in her befuddled mind. Then she began to giggle, God I can't believe I did that, playing up to him and telling them I had the virus. It sure surprises me what a person will do when their scared. I'd better get out of here before something else happens.

When she had finally reached an area that she recognized she sat down on the nearest stoop to catch her breath, head down in her hands, she was still panting and puffing when she looked up and saw Bobby headed her way.

"Oh shit, Just what I need, that asshole bugging me, ain't i got enough trouble with out him making it worse?"

Here again her mind went back to the moment and she relived the whole scene.

"Hi little lady, I was looking for you to see if you would like to have dinner with me," Bobby added, "nothing fancy just Pizza and a Coke"

"I just lost my appetite. Two me attacked me while I was walking on Clark Street, they dragged me into an alley and were going to rape me! So the last thing I need is Pizza and a Coke."

"You need a protector, someone they don't dare mess with. Theres a lot of dangerous people out there and I don't mean just men."

"I suppose your telling me that's you, just how the hell you going to protect me from trash like that?"

Bobby smiled and said, "You'd be surprised how much leverage I have when I need it."

"leverage," questioned Edna Sue, "what is that and how will it help me?"

"First of all I put out the word that you

belong to me, then I pay a few people to watch out for you." Bobby smiled and continued with his sales pitch. "Hell I got me five other girls that I protect for a price and I can do the same for you. All it costs you is thirty dollar a month, a dollar a day and I see that no harm comes to you."

Shaking her fist in Bobby's direction she screamed, "You're a pimp! A goddamn pimp. I thought you were a friend."

"Get real women, nobody does nothing for nothing, not in this town anyway."

"You can go to hell, I ain't gonna give you any money so you can put that in you pipe and smoke it! A goddamn pimp, thats what I choose for a friend, shows you how screwed up I am."

"You will be dammed glad to have me around when the going gets tough, you can bet your ass on that." Bobby dry washed his hands and added a sneer. " Listen bitch, It won't be long before you will be begging me to help."

"Go protect your women big man, I got better things to do and they don't include you!"

"We'll see little girl, by the way how old

are you? I'd say you're about fourteen or fifteen at most, maybe I'd better contact Social Service and have them check you out."

"I'm old enough to be on my own. What do you think they would say if I told them that you raped me or didn't you think of that?"

"Who's gonna believe a runaway, especially if I tell them that you've been turning tricks in the neighborhood. My old man knows all the cops on this end of town, how many cops do you know?"

"None and that's the way I want to keep it. Edna Sue's heart was pounding from the threat of being turned in to the cops and being sent back home to hell. "Just leave me alone and I'll pretend the rape didn't happen."

"Sure, sure, I guess we could do that. We could be friends you know, no strings attached." Agreed Bobby, All the while planning his next assault on her weakest point. She will come around soon. I wasn't sure how old she was but that jab I threw about her age sure hit home. Gotta keep that in mind for later use.

She had seen the way Bobby was processing the information she had let slip and knew that she could never trust him, but she pretended to believe him when he said they could be friends.

Dear God she was so hungry she felt faint. I'll let him buy me a pizza and coke, she decided, but the coke better be in an unopened can, no more drugging me to get into my pants.

They made their way to Sammy's Pizza Palace, and taking a table by the door they stared at the menu board over the counter. When Sammy spotted her and who she was with he slowly shook his head. With resignation he had come over to take their order. "Hello little lady and how are you today?" Sammy completely ignored the furious Bobby who was staring at Sammy with contempt welling out of every inch of his being.

"How is job hunting coming along? Have you had any bites yet? Shouldn't be too hard for a beauty like you," Staring straight at Bobby, he added, "that's if you keep your nose clean and watch who you hang around with."

Bobby saluted Sammy with his raised middle finger and smiled a vicious smile.

Sammy continued wiping the table, his

hands roughly hitting the aggravated Bobby's shoulder with the wet rag. "You know, I have a friend who could give you a couple of jobs, small time at first but you will need pictures to show clients."

Bobby chimed in saying he would get all the pictures she'd need. She didn't need help from strangers.

Sammy shrugged his shoulders and murmured, "Just trying to help," and he went behind the counter to get their pizza.

An angry Edna Sue was just about to set Bobby straight about who was going to take her pictures when she noticed the police officer standing outside the window staring at her as if he recognized her.

He scratched his head, unfolded a white piece of paper, staring at it for the longest time, shook his head before he refolded it and stuck it in his pocket. Opening the door he shouted, "Hi Sammy, hows it hanging?"

"Low Pete, very low, same as it always is," Sammy gave that same answer, every day of every month of every year of his life. Taking the hot pizza pan from the oven he took it toward Edna Sue and Bobby

Pete had been on this beat ever since he

joined the force. He knew all his people, as he called them, and they knew him. His instinct was telling him that something was wrong with this picture. *What was this child doing with that asshole, Bobby?*

Pete scanned the rest of the folks sitting at the counter and then he turned toward the table where Bobby and the girl were sitting eating their food.

"Hi there Bobby, just what the hell have you been to, beat up any old ladies lately? I heard you moved on to bigger and better things like running whores for your living. How does it feel to have girls supporting your ass?"

Pete came over to the table and dropped down in the chair opposite Edna Sue.

"Hey kid, how old are you and where you from? Does your parents know you hang out with pimps?"

"I'm eighteen," she answered . I don't need anyone's permission to hang out with who I chose."

"Got any ID little girl?"

"No," Edna Sue answered, "it was stolen from me."

"Well little Missy, I think I'd better check you out. What's your name honey, where you from?

My guts telling me you got something to hide. Won't answer hey, well thats okay, the JDH has lots of room for a smart ass like you. If you are eighteen and have a job, some place to live we'll find out. If not you gotta move on, we got enough whores in this neighborhood already!"

"Whats the JDH?" The terrified girl asked.

"That is the Juvenile Detention Home, a place where they know how to deal with whores and streetwalkers. Just wait and see what you will learn in that fine institution."

Sammy had walked over and tried to convince Officer Pete that he should let Edna Sue finish her pizza before he took her in, but he had no luck. Pete had grabbed the shaking girl and shoved her out the door into the waiting arms of another cop who had been waiting outside.

She was taken before a judge who placed her into the custody for further investigation by the juvenile court. The girl refused to give them any information, not even her first name. The court officer placed her in a holding cell until she could be transferred to the home for wayward girls and runaways.

As soon as she had arrived at the building where she would spend a week of hell, she asked to take a shower, wash her clothes, and have some food.

"Honey," retorted a women dressed in the drab gray of a state uniform, "You sure can have a shower and we will even give you a nice clean uniform to wear, does that suit your highness?

Because of the color of the dress she was wearing, and the fact that she refused to give her name, all the matrons began calling her Orange. Edna Sue liked the nickname and decided to keep it as her professional name when she became a model. A lot of models only had one name, she reasoned, besides if she gave these people her real name they would send her back home to be used by that old man who calls himself her father.

Here I will be known as Orange, I might as well get used to my new name

She had been scared that first night in JDH, huddling in the hard narrow cot on a stiff chlorine smelling sheet, her taunt body covered with a khaki colored blanket that scratched every time she moved. The shower had been ice cold, the lava soap that she was given would not lather. Try as she might all she could get the soap to do is scratch her skin with its grainy cleanser. The rancid smelling shampoo could not erase the foul smell of the disinfectant and liquid that was used to delouse her was part of her introduction into the juvenile home. Next she was taken into a large room, directed toward a metal table and given a metal plate filled with something resembling stew. Chunks of grease floated on the lukewarm food but Edna Sue knew she needed something to calm her empty, growling stomach. She had spooned in a few bites of the unappetizing concoction, felt her guts settle down and she planned on leaving the rest for the mice she'd seen sneaking around the dinning area. Even here her plans were foiled, she was required to turn in her empty dish when she left the area. Scrapping the cold wet mess into a garbage can located near the door, she stacked her greasy plate on top of the pile of other greasy plates.

    As she had lain shaking in her cot she could hear the soft sobbing of a lonely sounding soul, in the jet black night. Suddenly a hand reached under her cover, her heart stopped for a minute, what was going on here, she screamed and sat up in bed. Her bed began to shake and rise slowly. A raspy voice whispered, "One of these nights, I'll be back for you, sweet meat. Yer gonna get the fucking of your life!"

    Clutching the edge of the metal bed her stomach began to convulse. She could no longer hold down the greasy food that she had eaten, the vomit hurled across her bed onto the bed next to her. The girl who was sleeping in the bed came out swinging. Screaming obscenities, fist flying, she flew onto Orange's bed.

    Bright lights came flashing on; standing in the doorway was the biggest women Orange had ever seen. "Alright you bitches, you know I don't hold with no funny business on my shift, get back to your own bed and I better not hear a peep out of any of ya. Remember not a peep!"

    Orange looked around the dorm, everyone was in their bed, so who was messing with her? Her eyes made contact with a tough looking girl on the other side of the room and her body went rigid. The big rough looking girl with short black hair, cold black eyes and a slash across her cheek was smiling. That smile sent chills up and down Orange's spine. The lights went out but she could only sit and shake, her lids refused to close and she peered into the black hole of hell.

In the blackness of the night Orange had heard someone giggle and say, "Peep, peep."

After she heard the peeps, her heart stopped racing, she felt her eyes closing, she didn't even fight the sleep that she so badly needed.

Again she was back in the past. Was the drugs doing this she wondered as she gave in to the memories.

Orange was torn from her dreams of flight by the clang of the huge metal doors being thrown open. She had dreamed she was in France and the whole world was begging for her to honor them with her presence.

"Showers and breakfast in ten minute," shouted the small black matron. lining up they and were handed clean uniforms that they were to wear at all times. Single file they were led into the showers, dashing through the cold hall way they each went under the corroded spigots spouting ice cold, gray water. The bars of gray green soap smelled of disinfectant and still refused to lather. Orange had hoped the different colored soap meant it was a better kind, gentler and more foamy.

She did her best to wash every part of her body with that poor excuse for soap in the short time they were allowed. Finding no towel to dry her freezing flesh, she put her clothes on over her damp body.

A whistle blew and the girls lined up in single file to go to the dinning room for breakfast. They each stood behind a chair until the whistle blew again and the the inmates sat down. Big Bertha sat down next to Orange, pressed her ample hip against the stunned girl. Touching Orange's hand, she grinned a wide smile that showed teeth green from lack of hygiene. Orange wanted to shrink up and blow away from this creature, but she knew that if she flinched Big Bertha would win. She turned to face the enemy. Staring hard into the cold black eyes of the menacing girl, she said in a low, threatening voice, "Git the hell away from me before I cut your tits off, you ain't got no use for them anyway. If you ever bother me again your ass is dead. Got it?"

Shocked, Big Bertha stood up and moved

to another table, but her eyes never left Orange's face. Hate, fear, and cunning played across the pursuer's countenance. Nobody had ever defied her before and she didn't like the bitter taste defeat left in her mouth

    Orange knew that here was a person that she would have to keep an eye on at all times. She prayed that she would get out of here before Big Bertha caused her any more trouble.

    After breakfast the group was herded into a gymnasium like room with a stage at one end. The girls separated into smaller cliques and each headed for what was obviously their own part of the room. Orange sat down at the far right of the stage, away from all the groups. She could feel all eyes on her but she refused to look at anyone.

    As most courageous animals do when threatened, Orange held her her head high, shoulders wide, making herself look as formidable possible in the face of the enemy. She could smell the fear and tension in the room, thick enough to crowd Orange into a corner of her mind where she could escape the nameless threat. Her shoulders ached and her gut went all queasy from the tension, she didn't know what to expect next. She did know that she had to escape from the clutches of the girl with the shocking needs.

One of the girls who had been huddled in the closest group walked over and asked Orange if she wanted to join them.

Thank God, she thought, at least I will have someone to talk to. "Sure I would. By the way what do you do all day in this mansion by the sea?"

The girls who were waiting to see if she would accept their invitation, began to giggle, then they roared until their eyes watered. They felt a new found freedom. The stress of living in this prison like atmosphere had beaten down, these escapees from the life that had been thrown at them.

Orange glanced up and there was the dead looking eyes staring at her from across the room. She felt chills invade her body and she knew that her enemy was waiting for the right moment to strike. She no longer felt like wisecracking. The others in the group sensed the change in Orange's attitude and quickly settled down on the floor in a loose oval, as though they were circling the wagons.

Bottoms, numb from sitting on hard wood

floors, they talked. Some told stories of home, some talked of people they missed and some said nothing. Most had been sexual assaulted by father, brother, uncle, or family friend. As they shared their stories a familiar theme ran through them all. Alcohol, drugs,.and greed were the main reasons that most of these girls were here. Not drug use on their part, but on the part of their caretakers. They were betrayed by the very people who were supposed to love and protect them from a dangerous world.

    Orange realized for the first time that she wasn't the only one in this world with the horrible secret of abuse. She finally had someone she could talk to, someone who would know exactly what she meant when she said, "I feel like I'll never be clean, never wash away the filth." These girls would recognize her feelings of shame.

    One of the girls from another group, got up and moved to a spot where she could be alone. Hugging herself, she began to croon a hauntingly beautiful melody. Orange could hear the tears in the girl's lament. The strangely beautiful sound that issued from the girl's heart told her story, though she'd spoken not a word. The mournful yearning tore at the hearts of the listeners, filling their hearts with an inescapable sadness.

Desperately, Orange thought, *I have to get out of here before I lose my mind. Surround by girls who were in the same situation as she, but Orange never felt so alone in her miserable life.* She began to cry silently inside. It would never do to let anyone see her show emotion or weakness.

The main meal of the day was a combination of lunch and dinner, and thats exactly what it looked like. The food was thrown together, heated in a big pot and scooped out by a metal ladle onto a metal plate. JDH was embossed in the center like a stamp on her life, a label telling everyone what she was, a slut. Her outlook couldn't be darker. *Don't they ever let you forget that your lock up?*

On the third day, after two sleepless nights, the matron came to tell Orange that her parents were here to take her home. She wondered how they had found her so quickly, and why they had even bothered to come for her. Dad wanted her there but mom sure didn't.

She followed the matron down a long hall that smelled of disinfectant, urine, and god knows what else. She entered into a room with tables and chairs lined along one side of the wall. A strange man and women sat at the first table smiling in her direction. The man, stood and put out his cigarette, motioning for her to sit, he thanked the matron and sat back down at the table.

Who the hell are these people, she asked herself, and why would they say they are my parents?

Slowly sitting down, Orange asked, "Who are you and why did you tell them that you were my parents?"

The thin, bald man sneered at her saying,"For money, what else?"

The obese women with bright red hair giggled at her husbands words and added, "Besides we always wanted a child and now we have one. We named you Jennie, ain't that a nice name?"

"Who paid you to pretend you are my parents and where did you get the proof that you're my parents?"

"Oh honey, Bobby's took care of the miner details, he knows a guy who can make anything and make it look legit"

"Well I'm not ready to be one of Bobby's women yet," Orange explained, "I will wait to see what other choices I have."

Standing up abruptly she shouted, "Matron I don't even know these people , please take me back to my quarters."

The smelly old man placed his mouth next to Orange's ear and snickered, "Bobby's not paying us enough to kiss your ass, so you better make up your mind by our next visit or you can rot in here for all I care."

"Now honey," cautioned the man's wife, "you know I always wanted a kid, don't piss her off so's she won't want to come with us," the women begged her angry mate.

"Goddammit old woman, ya know we can't keep her anyhow. Why would you want her? Besides she's too damn mouthy for me. I like the quiet ones."

"Now pa , the women arbitrated, "you know you can't pick and choose your children, you get what comes along."

The man flew into a rage, jumped up flinging the table, chair and ashtray onto the marble floor. Grabbing his wife by the hair, he jerked her to the locked metal door. Shouting at the matron who had stepped out into the hall to give them privacy, he apologized for his wild behavior, blaming his frustration on Orange.

The matron shook her head and told the supposed parents, "I've seen this happen a thousand times before, she will come around after a few more weeks in this place.

"Kid," she directed her comments in Orange's direction, "you won't be getting out anytime soon unless you get released to your parents. You can take my word for that!"

Back in the gym, going over the meeting of the strange couple, Orange decided it would be safer here than out on the street with her "New Parents." Dear God why do people like that exist, she questioned.

Shanna, her first real friend she had made in the juvenile home, sat shaking her head sympathetically. Orange felt the sobs rising in her chest, she fought to quell the tide of hopelessness that seemed to invade her whole body.

Shanna was in the same boat as Orange, she too had been picked up for prostitution, she also had met Bobby when she first arrived in town and liked him immediately. She didn't find out for a couple of weeks that she was just part of his harem. She said her heart was broken when he told her what she had to do. He had explained to her that working the streets was her way of showing him how much she loved him. He told her that she was his special girl and would only be on the streets until another girl came along to take her place. His explanation was, he had many obligations to take care of and must have a certain amount of money coming in every day to meet them. He had promised Shanna that as soon as another girl as good looking as she came along he would put her on Shanna's corner and she could stay home and take care of him and only him.

    When Shanna had first told her about Bobby, accusing words jumped to Orange's lips, she started to tell Shanna that she knew Bobby too and that she also knew what he was, but she seen the love and trust in Shanna's eyes when she spoke his name. Orange bit her tongue and waited for a better time to tell the girl that her love was a pimp and an asshole who was using her. He never planned on taking Shanna off the streets until she was too old to be of any use to him or any other man.

    Orange tried to change the subject several times. She was getting nauseous when Shanna told her about her plans for the future with Bobby. The love smitten girl could only dream of the day when she would be Bobby's wife.

    That asshole has really sold her a bill of goods, thought Orange, I hope I'm not that dense.

    Orange suddenly felt something threatening her space. She remembered what her mother would say, that someone had just walked over her grave. Dear God thats an awful thought when your young and alive.

    Across the room was Big Bertha, her aggressor from the other night staring at her with a slight smile on her face. Her uniform was hiked up until everyone could see that she wore no under clothes and that she was well aware that her huge behind was exposed to whoever wanted to look.

    The others in the room were watching through side wise glances, not daring to look directly at Orange and her antagonist.

    Just then the matron slammed into the room announcing the noon meal was ready and they better line up for the march to the dinning room. Orange breathed a sigh of relief, another showdown averted, but she knew that the reprieve couldn't last forever. She was amazed how quickly she had adapted to the regimen of the Juvenal Detention Home, or JDH as the inmates called it. She was thankful for the interruption that had saved her from another confrontation with the determined Big Bertha.

    The meal was a tense affair with all the other girls on edge from the near miss with Big Bertha and the impending conflict. Orange had tried to act as though she didn't have a care in the world but her quivering voice and shaking hands gave her away. The girls who had befriended her were too afraid to give her any support other then sit at the table with her. When the meal was over and they had each done the chores assigned them, some mopping shiny tile floors, and a couple of the girls were given the job of feeding the younger children who were unable to feed themselves. Orange was assigned to feed Emily, an eight year old Downs Syndrome child with bright tufts of black hair on her huge misshapen head, and small green eyes that stared at nothing.

While feeding the empty body that drooled out what food was not shoved directly into her mouth, Orange couldn't control her tears. A slow rage was building in her mind, how could they do this to a poor helpless child? When she got back to the gym area she asked the others if they had seen Emily and did they know why she was here. Sure they answered; "Her father is a crack head and he was selling her to other crack heads for rocks."

"No," Orange screamed, "not that little baby, my God she must be torn to pieces. Why is she here?"

"She is a prostitute in the eyes of the law, besides there ain't no other place for her," piped up one of the younger girls, " at least here she's safe, she's got food, and ain't nobody bothering her."

"Where is her mother? Why isn't she with her mother," sobbed Orange. "Dear God, I gotta get out of here before I lose my mind."

"Ya right!" Shanna predicted, "The only way your gonna get outta here is when your parents come to get you and the judge says so. If I was you I'd jump at the chance to get out with our friend Bobby's help or your going to be here until your eighteen. Besides you know Big Bertha's set her mind on you for her girlfriend and she is gonna keep it up till she wins." Shanna shuddered as she spate out her prophecy to a very frightened Orange.

"I could take a chance with those people I guess," reasoned Orange. "I wouldn't have to stay with them after I'm out. I can get away from them real easy and it would be better then staying in here."

Maggie the matron smirked at the seemingly penitent girl as Orange asked when her parents were coming to visit again.

"Two days till visiting day," answered the matron with a superior attitude. "Get your shit together and maybe you will get released, but then maybe not." A small laugh escaped her cruel mouth as she winked at Orange.

She'd seen enough of these floozies come though the doors not to recognize a slut when she saw one. Why look at the way she teased Big Bertha. Orange was always flaunting her cute little ass in front of Bertha. Maggie had been there in Bertha's place once and nearly lost her job because of it. Now she limited her pursuit of females to lonely nights in bars where other lonely females went to ease the loneliness.

Sure they weren't the love of her life that she was searching for, but they kept the wolf at bay.

Orange could do nothing but ignore Maggie's behavior toward her. She tried to explain that she was ready to go home with her parents and behave herself, but the matron was off in her own little world where Orange had no voice.

Two whole days in which to make plans. Those two days dragged into what seemed like a week, with no more incidents with Big Bertha. That worried Orange. Bertha wasn't the kind to give up easily, she only hoped that she would be out of here before the determined girl could exact her vengeance. Maybe she doesn't know I'm leaving. I'll bet that that is what it is, she thinks she has all the time in the world, well let her think that, it'll work for me.

Visiting day finally came and Orange was ready to jump at the chance to accept those people as, 'her ever loving parents', but no one came to claim her.

The matron had come with a list of names

for visitors; Orange's name was not on the list.

"Damn them, where are they! How am I going to get out now," the frantic girl berated herself. "I blew it, I should have said they were my parents when they first came, now I'm screwed!"

Maggie, the matron with her own cross to bear, came into the gym and pointed at Orange. "You go to court in an hour, so pick up your stuff and come with me. Don't just sit there move your hind-end when I speak."

A million questions were chasing each other through the startled girl's brain. What do I do now, what am I thinking, what can I do. I didn't break the law did I? Is it against the law to run away? Oh shit, I got no choice just go along with what ever happens. She picked up the comb that Shanna had given her. It had half its teeth missing, but to Orange it was precious. It was the first thing someone had given her without wanting something in return.

The belligerent Maggie led the confused child through a maze of halls into another part of the building that was called the waiting area.

The room was huge, with high windows lining one wall; plain wooden chairs lined the opposite wall. Nothing broke the great expanse of wall at either end of the chamber. Every sound was amplified.

Orange shuffled her feet and the faint noise in that huge empty room sounded like a herd of stampeding cattle. Her mind wandered back to her home and the situation that forced her to leave in the first place. Thoughts of better days came flashing into her mind and passed just as quickly. Why couldn't I stay young, not grow up pretty enough to tease my daddy. Thats when it started. I got my curse, it was as though my daddy needed that signal and couldn't leave me alone. What is it that makes a man want to do that to you even if you are his own child. Is there some kind of scent they can smell. Dogs breed that way but not people, or at least I don't think so.   Ain't they ever going to come for me?

This room is freezing. If they think sitting for hours in this cold empty room is supposed to get a person thinking about her situation, its working, but the only thing I regret is getting caught. I'll work hard to see that never happens again, if I ever get out of this mess.

Lonely and frightened Orange had hugged herself for warmth and waited.

When at long last the court clerk called out the name Jennie, Orange didn't respond. She wasn't used to being called Jennie, the name the hired parents had given her. The clerk repeated the name for a second time and asked her if she was trying to be a smart ass for not answering.

Standing before the judge, Orange had tried to look humble, but it was against her very nature to grovel before anyone.

The judge spoke to the bogus parents completely ignoring the proud young women before him. With distaste in his eyes he ordered the family to get counseling, attend family guidance seminars, and report to the court after they have resolved their differences. He had seen this same situation every day for the twenty years that he had been a judge. If there was an easy way to mend families he wasn't aware of it. Arresting the runaway wasn't the answer, shoving the child back into the home where the problems began didn't solve anything either. Maybe counseling would help but he couldn't see any future for children raised by parents who just didn't give a shit. Bitter, yes, but each day that he entered the court room he hoped there would be some kind of break. A law, a proclamation, a damn miracle that would put these children first, some new solution that would save the children.

The judge addressed Orange for the first time, "Young lady. if I see you in my court again for this or any other infraction I will put you away for a long time. Go home and try to get along with your parents, they are doing the best they can for you and you must give them a chance. Now get out of my court!"

When the bogus parents and Orange came out of the court house and into the sunlight, Bobby joined them. Taking Orange's arm, he steered her to a waiting cab. Turning to the hired parents he hissed, "I paid you enough for this job so get your own ride."

Jumping into the cab, Bobby grabbed the shaking girl by the arm, twisting it slowly he warned, "You're in my world now baby, so shape up or else."

Orange sat very still, her mind whirling in utter confusion. What am I going to do now. Should I tell Bobby to go to hell or just play along until I can figure something out.

Orange had smiled weakly and nodded her head, slumping down further into the seat, trying to give Bobby the impression of defeat.

A sly look flitted across Bobbie's face and he flashed a winning smile at the suddenly cowed young lady. *I got her by the short hairs now,* He silently gloated.

As the cab had pulled up in front of her rooming house, Bobby turned to her and told her that he wanted her out on the streets working tonight. She was out there until she earned at least two hundred dollars for each day. He reminded Orange with another twist of her arm that she owed him a lot of money. He had hired the couple that pretended that they were her parents and the forged papers didn't come cheap. He wanted his money first then she could worry about her own problems.

"Don't even think about skipping out, I have a lot of friends in this neighborhood and they all know you belong to me."

She had gotten out of the cab and made her way up the stairs to her rooms, unlocking the door she had stood on the threshold and whispered, "Home at last."She dragged her tired body over to the bed and sank down onto the lovely bright spread that was covering her most prize possession, the gaily painted orange metal bed. Head hanging, heart empty, she mumbled, "A hooker is not what I came here to be." The sick feeling in her stomach invaded her heart. *O god, She thought, what have I done to deserve this? I'm so scared, what will I do, how can I get away from Bobby when almost all of my money is gone and the rent is only paid for another two weeks. Can I do that, hook to pay him back and get him off my back? If I work real hard I can hold some money back for a stash and Bobby won't know anything about it, then I can get out of here and make a new start.*

    Her decision was made; she had set the wheels in motion for another drastic change in her demoralizing life.

    Orange had prepared herself for the ordeal by dressing with great care, ironing the wrinkles from her beloved orange dress with sweaty hands, caressing the silky feel of the dress she wore as a badge of freedom, she brushed her hair, painted on a bright orange smile, flicked her hair over her shoulder and went down the stairs to the street corner that

Bobby had assigned her.

Her first client had been a businessman who had was cruising by just as Orange took her place on the corner. He was so taken with her innocence that he paid her the fifty she had asked for, and tried to get her promise to save time for him on Mon. Wed. and Fridays at three o-clock. She agreed but had no intention of keeping that promise.

The clerk at the liquor store down the street sold her the bottle of wine with out even looking up from his racing form. She fortified herself with a sip of wine after her first encounter. It did help dull the accusations that were resounding in her mind, but she also knew that she had to do this for a few more weeks so she had another sip of the magic elixir that helped cover her revulsion and went back to work.

By midnight she had serviced six men and had three hundred dollars tucked in her bra. Enough, she thought, taking the half empty bottle back to the room with her. When she reached home she could see that the lights in the room were on. Running up the stairs she flung open the door and there lay Bobby, naked, sprawled on her bed with a young girl

Orange's age or younger.

"Meet Susan," Bobby drawled, "she will be sharing this room with you."

"No!" Screamed Orange, "you can't just drag someone in here and tell me they can stay! This is my place, I paid for it and you can't take my home away from me!"

Bobby had whirled off the bed, grabbed a handful of Orange's hair and forced her to her knees, twisting the arm that she had raised to defend herself, he told her, "You bitch, don't you ever tell me what I can and can't do. I own you! If I tell you to eat shit you will do it and ask for more. Have you got that? Where's my money, you better have it or you're out on the street again until you get it?"

"Yes, yes I got it," Her head bowed so he couldn't see the loathing in her eyes. She whispered as she crumbled before Bobby's brutality, "I got enough for tonight."

Susan had smiled shyly at the kneeling girl and offered her hand to help Orange rise from that humiliating position.

Pushing Susan back on the bed Bobby said, "Let that smart ass get up by herself. Both of you better get it through your little bee bee brains that whatever I say goes. Now sweet meat, get back down here and let me finish what that bitch broke up."

Edna Sue, now known as Orange lay on the floor looking forlorn and beaten, but inside her mind was running full tilt, plotting a way to escape from that pig Bobby.

When Bobby had finished using Susan he dressed and left the tiny apartment, shouting over his shoulder, "I want both off you out on the street at five o'clock tomorrow for the office trade."

Bobby had been mechanical in the use Susan's body, leaving her shattered. "I thought he loved me," she sobbed.

Orange remembered pulling herself up, locking the door and turning to the sobbing girl and telling her that Bobby didn't love anyone or anything. "Bobby doesn't know the meaning of love! I'm going to get away and you should too before he kills us both."

"I can't leave, Bobby needs me. He promised me that I would only have to help him for a little while then we could be together. Just the two of us forever."

"What in hell does it take to make you see him for what he is?" Orange shrugged her shoulders and went to the cupboard to find anything to ease her gnawing stomach. "Oh well, you do what ever you want to do but I'm out of here."

"Where can you go, Susan asked, "Orange, he has friends everywhere?"

"I don't know, " hissed Orange, but I do know that I didn't come this far just to end up hooking for some guy who's too lazy to earn his own living. I gotta get away that's all there is to it!" The crackers that were left from her first meeting with Bobby were still in the cupboard and when she dug into the small cluttered storage space, out jumped a rat! Gone was her hunger. Sweating, shaking like a leaf in the wind, she dragged herself to the bed. Flopping down on the rumpled spread she wondered if she could ever make it in this cold, brutal town.

She could smell the rancid odor of Bobby and his cheap aftershave mixed with the smell of the men that she had entertained in the street. Stomach rolling, she jumped up, stripped the sheets and bedspread from her once cherished metal scroll work bed, threw them in the corner and lay down on the ugly stained mattress. Tomorrow she would burn the sheets and spread that she had so carefully chosen for her new home.

Susan had crept hesitantly over to where Orange lay, she reached out and touched Orange's face with her index finger."Are you all right? Is it alright if I stay here tonight, I don't have anywhere else to go."

"Yes, you can stay." Orange rolled over and made room on the bed for the girl who was just as trapped as she.

Orange spent the next two years as a working girl and was able to save very little money. Tommy always seemed to know when she had hidden some and beat her until she gave it to him. She went from booze to drugs just to keep from losing her mind during those horrible years and Tommy was more than glad to provide the heroin for her.

"Fate had taken over. Orange became pregnant in the beginning of her third year on the street. Orange was much too young and not streetwise enough to realize that one in ten thousand hard working girl makes it as a model in the big city and then only through luck and knowing important people who can put her in the right place at the right time, but she still hung on to her dream.

For every girl who makes it to the top,

thousands fall by the wayside and men like Bobby are there waiting to pounce on them as a means of support. You have to wonder if those men hate women so much that they force the women to degrade themselves to fulfill some agenda of revenge.

Tommy came and went as he pleased and began using her place as his packaging room. On this eventful night Bobby came in about midnight and he had another shifty looking individual with him. They sat down at the table and placed bags of white powder on the table between them. They were so busy they didn't hear the creeping noise in the hall.

Orange's mind came back from the past just in time to hear hammering on the door, a harsh voice shouted, "Police, open the door!"

Cops came bursting in pushing and shoving, fighting to be the first to enter the room. Bobby and his dealer sat paralyzed at the table filled to overflowing with packages of heroin. Small baggies half filled with empty promises lay spread over the whole table waiting for someone to reach out and grab the ring of death.

Jumping up from the table Bobby aimed a fist at one of the officers, he foolishly thought he could escape his capture. The dealer was doing the same,

Orange struggled to rise and escape the crush of men who were punching and battering each other. Her first thought was leave, her second thought was grab some of the baggies. Blue sleeved arms pulled her back onto the bed and pinned her there out of the way of the confusion.

The desperate girl felt an inner relief, She was caught, maybe now she could get help for her addiction. At first she hadn't wanted to admit that her dependency on the needle wasn't something she could control. Deluding herself into thinking that all she had to do was change her life style, get away from Bobby and she could kick the habit, she had been able to go on without the thoughts of suicide invading her mind. When she had finally faced the fact that she was hooked for life, she knew that she had to wait until after the child was born before she did anything to end this misery.

The young police officer named Kennith Hancock, who was holding the now compliant Orange out of harms way, knew the pain she was going through. His sister had fallen into that same trap and had never escaped. His mother and father were still grieving and blaming themselves. It had been three long years since she had overdosed and they still couldn't face the fact that she was really gone. Kennith knew that she had knowingly shot up too much of the drug as she had left a note with two words on it. The note had said, "I'm sorry." Kennith had found the note, picked it up and tucked it into his pocket, after all suicide was a sin for those of the Catholic faith. The desperate young officer was protecting his parents from the shame and agony knowing their little girl had taken her own life. An accident they could accept but not a planned taking of her own precious life. Officer Hancock did the second illegal thing in his life, he pulled Orange out of the apartment and dragged her down to the patrol car. Once there he told her to stay put and he would be right back. Going back to the apartment he motioned for Susan to follow him out the door. When they reached the street he told her to get out of town and don't come back. She lost no time in taking his advice.

 Taking Orange home to Mama was the most natural thing for Officer Hancock to do. His mother had lost a daughter and Orange needed a home. He prayed to God that he was doing the right thing.

Orange knew she would never have to worry about Bobby coming after her when he got out of jail and that was a relief to the frightened girl. Kennith had come home with the news that Bobby was found hanging in his cell on the Monday after he was arrested. His parents believed he was so filled with remorse over his misdeeds that he had taken his own life. The officers around the police station suspected it was retribution for past crimes against his fellow inmates.

No one pushed an investigation, one less trial, one less inmate, and a hell of a lot less paperwork!

The following year was a trip down an uneven road for the whole Hancock family, but with love and hope they all came through. A son was born to Orange and Grand ma and Grand Pa Hancock fell in love with the child on the day he was born.

One year later Kennith Hancock and Edna Sue were wed. Ma and Pa had taken her into their hearts and she had filled a small part of the empty space that had been left in their lives by their dead daughter. The baby Kenny

Jr. played with the hem of her lucky Orange dress as the preacher gave the blessings. The neighbors clapped hands as the happy couple kissed and little Kenny Jr. cooed and clapped his chubby little hand in delight.

The End
Ŏ

Once in a while fate gets it right!

B.N.

Me and My Shadow

Cassandra Jenkins stared into the gilt mirror that hung over her dressing table and saw a shy girl of eighteen, pretty but not exceptional looking. Mama had always said she was beautiful but all mothers say that. The horned rimmed glasses she always wore hid her large, lovely gray eyes, providing a barrier for her to hide behind. The sever hairstyle she'd affected did nothing to enhance the worlds image of the lonely girl. She alone knew how ugly she was inside.

Cassandra had moved out of her parent's home as soon as she could afford the rent on this one room studio apartment, hoping that a change of environment would open new worlds to her. She yearned for the exhilarating feeling of being worshiped by someone who would burst into her dull world, scoop her up and transport her to paradise.

She spent most of her nights home listening to the radio or television instead of being out in the world interacting with others. As she listened to the announcers telling her about all the exciting things happening to famous people. Her imagination led her to wonderful places, rubbing shoulders with beautiful people and falling in love with the perfect man.

Right after graduation from high school Cassandra had applied for and been hired by a small book store in a large mall on Saginaw's north side. The store had just enough costumers to stay in business but it never was so busy that Cassandra didn't have time to daydream about some of the beautiful patrons and wish she could trade places with those glamorous, successful women.

On this particular Saturday morning while she was busy cataloging a batch of new books, a lovely young women came into the shop searching for a certain book that had out of print for some time. She asked Patrica

Brown, the store manager to please locate it for her and she gave Patrica her name and number.

Patrica not being in one of her rare good moods, tossed the slip in the trash and forgot about it.

Waiting until Patrica went for her second coffee break, Cassandra picked the slip of paper containing the girl's name and number out of the waste basket and filled out a search slip for the book the girl was searching for.

Cassandra watched the incoming mail for any information on the book and found none.

Why, she wondered, *would the girl want to read a book about an old Indian cemetery, Cemetery of the Lost, was the name of the book and the synopsis said it was fiction based on fact. Strange that she would be interested, maybe I should read it too.*

She began to wonder where the girl lived, she had the address, tonight she could check it out. Nothing good on T.V. anyway.

Cassandra took a cab to the address on the slip of paper she had rescued from the trash and sat still staring at the building until the cab driver shouted, "You gonna get out or what? Lady I ain't got all night!"

Heart pounding, hands shaking, Cassandra paid the cab driver and stepped out into the dark street.

She lives here, She might be in her apartment right now getting ready for a fabulous night out on the town. I wonder if she has a date for tonight, of course she would, she's beautiful.

Cassandra watched the building until the rain started and she could no longer bear the pain of being left out in the cold, away from this special girl.

Her work days were full of anticipation for the incoming mail, the phone calls from the girl, and her own secret visits to the girl's apartment building.

Cassandra spent many a cold night hiding in a doorway watching the girl come home from dates with a well-dressed, handsome young man.

The radio no longer interested her, T.V. was boring, why watch the beautiful people on the tube when she could watch the real live person when ever she wanted to. Her days and nights were filled with the girl from the store, when she wasn't watching, she was dreaming of the two of them together, friends, close enough to be sisters. Her life took on new meaning.

She now had a purpose in life, she began to wear her hair in the same style as the girl from the store, she re-evaluated her own wardrobe and found it wanting. The shopping trip for new clothes took a big chunk out of her savings but she didn't care, it was for Linda.

There ! She'd done it, she'd said it out loud! She had found out the girl's name when she first began to worry about the book, but she had never dared say it out loud before, afraid that if she said it out loud it would some how jinx her dream. The freedom to finally say Linda's name out loud made it perfect and true. They were friends!

On her next day off after watching Linda's building for a week, she followed Linda to find out where she shopped for her stunning outfits. Finding some of the same clothes as Linda wore on a sale rack made Cassandra's day off perfect.

She had watched Linda one morning after church, her church not Linda's. Linda didn't attend church or at least not that Cassandra could find out. Cassandra decided, *if no church is good enough for Linda, then it is no church for me either.*

The other clerks who mostly worked part time in the store began to notice Cassandra's change in hair style, dress, and the faint blush of makeup on her smiling face. They began teasing her about having a secret lover. Patrica, the manager even asked Cassandra if she had moved in with this mysterious man who put that blush on her cheeks.

Cassandra was shocked at first, how dare they even think that about her, but as the thought burrowed into her mind it found a secure place and nestled in. She began to accept the idea that she could attract a lover, after all Linda had one so she could too! When she looked into the mirror now she saw a women who looked enough like Linda to be her sister.

She spent all her spare time following Linda from place to place, but she was always careful to stay out of sight or duck into a doorway whenever Linda glanced around.

While hiding behind a rack of sale

dresses, Cassandra happened to overhear Linda talking to the clerk. She was telling the girl that her name was Evelyn Linda Brown , but she had decided to go by the name Linda because it sounded prettier and she thought everyone should be able to choose what other people called them.

 She's right, why should I be weighed down with an old maid's name when I could have a beautiful, interesting name like Linda. But I really don't feel like a Linda, I do feel like a Cassie, how does that sound out loud? Cassie, Cassie, Cassie, I like it! It feels like me. That's who I'll be from now on!

 When she announced her name change to her fellow workers the next day the teasing became unbearable. She let her coworkers believe that there was indeed a secret lover. *It wasn't true,* she reasoned, *but it could be.*

 Linda was starting to go to some different places, she had even changed her clothing stores. Why? There were other small changes beginning to take place, the new boy friend that always seemed to be there, the new restaurants where she now had dinner, and she had begun going to St.

Mary's Church on Sunday morning. Why the change, what was happening in her life that makes her want to make all these changes.

Well if St. Mary's Church was good enough for Linda it's good enough for me. Cassie started attending church the following Sunday.

Cassie watched as Linda left the church, went to a waiting car and got in the passenger's side, Cassie's heart skipped a beat as she watched the car and Linda pull away.

Father Jack caught up with Cassie on the front steps of the church and welcomed her into the fold after the morning service. He asked her if she were new to the city or was she just visiting friends. She told she was searching for a new church home and she was visiting several churches in the area for a place where she could feel comfortable.

Cassie wished she didn't have to work for a living, it would give her more time to find out what Linda does all day. It seems like Linda doesn't have to work anywhere, she always has a lot of new clothes and an unending supply of money.

This new man in Linda's seems pretty

seedy looking; I wonder what she sees in him. Her other dates were always beautifully dressed, this one actually wore jeans and tennis shoes to the movie the other night. Cassie had sat a couple of rows behind them and heard his loud brash voice make some rude remark about the heroine. He's really uncouth, but Linda seems to like him so he must be all right.

 Patrica, pretending that she really gave a crap about Cassie's future with the company, went into her act as the gung-ho store manager and took Cassie back into her office for a little talking to about being late for work again.

 She said, "I don't know what has come over you but your job is suffering, is this man in your life taking up too much of your time or are you thinking of leaving us. Whatever the problem is you need to think of your future with this company. We cannot condone tardiness in our employees."

 Cassie was enraged by Patrica's stupid speech, she had worked for this company for six years and never been late or took time off until now. What did Patrica mean sticking her nose into Cassie's private life. She sure don't run the other employees lives, why does she think she can run mine?

She kept her mouth shut but her mind was on overload when she left Patrica's office. Working at top speed, mind seething, she found work that demanded physical exertion but left her brain free to scheme up some revenge.

Jerry one of the part timers who worked after school and Saturdays, accidentally bumped her while she was putting some books away and she viciously hit his arm with the feather duster she was carrying and she warned him not to touch her again.

Cassie couldn't wait for her shift to end, she was tired of taking this crap from these assholes, what did they know about her life? At Five thirty one she put her coat on, tucked her hair under the new hat that she and Linda had started wearing, and pushed her way to the front of the line. The two young part time clerks who were in the front of the line giggled at her enthusiasm, "She must be in a hurry to get home to Mr. Wonderful," commented one of the snickering teenagers.

Punching out on the time clock, Cassie practically ran out the door. Thank God I'm out of there, now I can breath, they're stifling me.

    I hope we go somewhere interesting tonight. I am getting so bored with those old movies she wants to see all the time, course just being with Linda is enough.

    Hurrying home to shower and change clothes Cassie was filled with a sense of freedom, she just knew it was going to be an exciting evening. She could feel it in her bones.

    When she got to Linda's apartment house she took her usual place behind a large shrub that stood near the entrance. It was a good thing she'd hurried, Linda was already coming out of the door, ready for her nightly shopping trip. What could she possibly need she has shopped every night since we started hanging out together. Well it's her choice if she likes to shop first, then go out on dates with those fantastic men she spends time with.

    Linda's going in to that hardware store, she's looking at guns, why would she be thinking of buying a pistol? Maybe that new man of hers is getting carried away and she's afraid of him. Well I better pick one up too; he could be dangerous to me as well since I'm Linda's best friend.

The clerk acted a little suspicious when she told him she wanted the same gun as her friend had just bought. "Lady why didn't you and your friend come together," the clerk asked.

Cassie told him it was none of his damn business, did he want to sell her a gun or not. She pitched a fit when he told her that there was a waiting period for guns.

"You didn't make Linda wait," Cassie accused the clerk. "However she got that gun is how I want one or I go to the police with what I know!"

"lady, she didn't get the gun yet but here is the same gun i showed her." The gun was a snubbed nose thirty-eight with two clips, price two hundred dollars. He reminded her that she would need a permit before she could carry a gun.

"I know, I know. Do you think I'm stupid or something?" Christ she was tired of dealing with these idiots, Linda doesn't have to take this shit so why should I.

Cassie filled out the papers the clerk had shoved in front of he, signed it with a flourish and tossed a twenty dollar bill at the startled man. "I will be back with my permit, in the mean time hold that gun for me."

"That's the same thing your friend did," smirked the clerk, "put money down and said she'd be back. I guess you two do know each other."

"Of course we do! We're best of friends," said the now smiling Cassie.

There, that just goes to show that the fates decree that we be the best of friends otherwise we wouldn't look alike and think alike, she told herself, as she followed a block behind Linda.

Linda turned into the brightly lite police station, went to the main desk and asked the desk Sargent where she could apply for a gun permit.

Cassie pretended she was reading the most wanted posters on the opposite wall. She smiled at Linda when Linda glanced her way. See, she told herself, she knows I'm here waiting for her like good friends do. She's lucky to have a best friend like me, I'm loyal to the core. We always go where she wants, never where I want to go, sometimes I get a little tired of her selfishness, but I always give in to her. That is part of being a best friend.

Oh, oh, it looks like she's in a hurry, I better wait to apply for my permit, it'll take too much time right now. I wonder what is so important that she can't wait until I fill out a few papers. You'd think she was the most important person in the world by the way she behaves. Oh well, off to another adventure, at least I'm never bored anymore like I used to be.

Linda grabbed a cab, gave her home address and sat back waiting for the cabbie to pull out into traffic.

Cassie whistled at a yellow cab going in the opposite direction, watched as he made a u turn pulled up to the curb and shouted, "where to Lady?"

The trip to Linda's apartment seemed to take twice as long as usual. Cassie suddenly remembered something very important. Today is our anniversary, Linda and I became best friends six months ago today. I wonder if she remembers, probably not, selfish people never remember what is important to others.

Wonder what happened to the jerk she

was dating, he hasn't been around for a few days, must have realized she was afraid of him and he flew the coop.

    Cassie watched as Linda got out of the cab and went into her building. I wonder if we're staying home tonight, I hope so my paycheck doesn't stretch very far. Work is such a drag now, how could I ever think it was fun and interesting? Thank God I've grown out of that notion because I think my days at the book store are numbered and I don't even care. Maybe I'll find out where Linda works and get a job there. I bet she write novels, or maybe human interest stories, something glamorous, I'm sure of that. I know she'd be happy to have me working closely with her. Best friends always want that.

    Today we get our guns. I can't wait to finish this dammed shift and get out into the real world.

    Funny when I picked up my gun the clerk mentioned that my friend and I look like sisters. I almost burst out laughing when he said she must like my taste because she was wearing the same pants suit as I had on. In fact he said he thought Linda had come back into the store for something she'd forgotten. I told him we always dress alike, even when we sleep; we wear the same nighties. Let him put that in his pipe and smoke it! Besides it was none of his dammed business we don't owe him any explanation for anything. I didn't know for sure if we wore the same things to bed, but now we do have all the same nightclothes. It had cost me a small fortune and i felt like a hooker when I first began wearing them, but now I'm used to them.

    Wonder what Linda does all day when I'm working, does she read, write or visit friends. I don't know if she has any female friends besides me, I must be her only one. This dammed cab seems to take forever to get to her apartment. Hey, I'm just in time, there she is now, coming home or leaving, I can't tell which. No, she's leaving in the cab. She's got to quit riding in cabs so much, I'm running out of money just trying to keep up with her.

    What in hell is she doing back at the police station, we got our permits last week, we don't need anything else.

    Hey, there's that seedy looking guy she

was dating, he must work here, don't tell me she's begging him to come back. Come on Linda, have a little class, never and I mean never beg a man to come back.

No, must be something else, he is filling out more papers. Wish I could get close enough to read what it is, maybe an accident report, wait maybe her apartment was robbed. i didn't see anyone strange around her place when I was there.

They're leaving together, her and jerk! Why in hell is she dragging jerk home with her, doesn't he have anything better to do then drive a women home from the station. Bet he doesn't haul the ugly ones home. Huh, our tax dollars at work!

What is he up to now, I didn't see him get out of the patrol car and here he is coming right at me. Well now I have a chance to tell him what I think of his taxi service!

"What do you mean asking me this question? Yes I do come this way quite often. Of course I have business in this neighborhood or I wouldn't be here. I'm visiting a friend and I have every right to be here! Okay, I'll be on my way but you're going to be sorry you harassed me when I report you to your superior, you can't treat a tax paying citizen that way."

So that's why Linda went back to the police station, to report a stalker and they thought it was me. Well we can straighten this mess out right now all Linda has to do is tell them that we are best friends. I can't figure out why she didn't tell them that in the beginning. She knows I would never hurt her, I love her. I want to be just like her and there she is turning her back on me. Worried about what that dammed jerk thinks about her no doubt. She keeps screwing around with the cops and she could lose her best friend.

That lieutenant said Linda, doesn't know me and she doesn't want to be friends with a stalker. Me a stalker, no way, I'm just a friend who helped her trace a book, and made sure she got it when no one else cared. I watched over her for months and now she tells the police I stalked her! Well I'll show her what stalking really is, she can't abandon me like this, we've been friends too long.

Dammit that jerk is there again tonight! Don't he ever go home? That's Okay, I have lots of time now that I got fired from the book store. It's all Linda's fault, she started this whole mess with her snooty ways and then pretending we weren't friends. I hated that dammed job anyway, especially after everybody started getting strange. They were jealous because I had a best friend and didn't need them anymore. I better get out of here before jerk sees me. I guess I could take in a movie. I get to pick which one I want to see, not forced to see something I don't like just because Linda wants to see it.

What a waste of time that movie was, a complete bust, I should have picked one Linda would like then my money wouldn't have been wasted. I need to talk to her and get things settled, we can't go on this way after all we are best friends.

Well what do you know the jerk is gone! I can let myself in, we can sit down and discuss this like best friends should.

My key won't work! What happened, it worked last week when I stopped in for a drink of water. She had the locks changed! God dammed her she is making things more difficult than they have to be. That bitch! I'll show her! Why does she have to jeopardize our friendship that way. She's making it impossible to be her friend. If that's what she wants then so be it.

Here comes jerk again, I'll bet she called him to protect her from me, her best friend. I'll let him think he's won and that I will stay away from now on, there's more than one way to skin a cat!

"What do you mean you'll lock me up for visiting my friend, how ridicules and they call this a free country! Okay, okay, I'm on my way, don't get your shorts in a knot! "

Did I really say that to him? Well, the one good thing that Linda taught me is how to stand up for myself. Now I have to come up with a plan to get Linda back on my side. She sure is fickle!

I should start carrying my gun again, it's getting so a girl isn't safe from jerks anymore. I'm going to give Linda one more chance to get this mess straightened out. If she doesn't think our friendship is worth saving then I will end it once and for all.

Linda's had her number changed! That bitch is really making it difficult, but she don't know who she is dealing with. I've lived with bigger mountains to climb. I can handle this too.

Another two weeks went by, the longest two weeks of Cassie's life. She tried to get interested in T.V. again but nothing tweaked her interest like thoughts of Linda, her dates, and her full life.

When Cassie thought enough time had passed that Linda had forgotten her annoyance with her supposed stalker, Cassie started watching the apartment house for Linda and her jerk friend. After watching for a couple of days she realized that Linda didn't live there anymore. A rage began to burn in her heart, she would find her and let her know how deeply she had hurt her best friend.

Watching the police station day and night for jerk to leave work, she waited. At last her vigilance paid off, jerk came out, jumped into a patrol car and headed out of town. Cassie hailed a cab and told the driver she was on a news story and she needed him to follow the cop car, but don't get too close.

At the Family Motel, just off the highway, jerk pulled in, parked in front of number10, knocked and Linda opened the door.

When jerk went inside, Cassie paid the cab driver, waited until he drove off and then she crept closer to the window of the room. There on the bed sat Linda dressed in nothing but robe and slippers.

Jerk sat in a chair across from her with a lecherous leer on his face.

The words, **He's going to hurt her,** marched through Cassie's brain. She pulled out her gun, steadied herself, planning to burst into the room, she fought the urge to scream as she pushed through the unlocked door.

The first shot hit her square in the chest, the second shot went through her left eye. Her last thoughts were, What an awful way to treat a best friend.

Linda told the reporters that she knew someone was stalking her for quite a while but she couldn't prove it. She had the feeling that someone had been in her apartment but nothing was missing. One morning before she left the flat she had put put a piece of lint on the top of the dresser, even wet it so it stuck to the top. When she came home later it was gone. Someone had dusted the whole top of the dresser, so now she knew. She'd seen the girl from the bookstore around but never in this world thought that sad little girl could be her stalker. The man at the hardware store had supplied her first clue when he asked about the strange women who always seemed to turn up right after she left the store. He said the women had wanted the same kind of gun as she bought, and she had always worn the same clothes as Linda had on.

    That is when Linda really got scared and contacted the police. She and the lieutenant had set this trap for the stalker never expecting it to work this soon, but it did.

    Cassie's former co-workers couldn't believe the story the news papers carried about the copycat stalker. They knew that Cassie had changed a lot but they thought it was because of a man, not because she wanted a new identity, or was obsessed with one of their customers.

    Linda had thought Cassie was gloomy, but beautiful, how sad that she wasn't happy being her self. "If I was as pretty as she was I would never have gone into hooking for a living, Linda lamented, "Some people have all the breaks!"

The End

Some folks are never satisfied!

B.N.

The strange tale of Sweet Boy began while I was searching through death records at the Court House in Bay City, Michigan. I ran across the record of an eleven year old boy who the records say was murdered by his step-mother. I could find no other information about this incident in either the news papers or the census records so my imagination built him a life. This story and all the other stories in this book are fiction based on facts gathered from the past.

BN

Sweet Boy

    Dawn broke the dark sky on the day that Steven Boyd Gilbert was born. Catherin Mae Gilbert lay exhausted and feverish from two long days of labor.   Eyes closed, mind racing, she fought to stay conscious. What in hell was she going to tell Henry? He was dumb but way too smart to believe this kid was his. Henry had gotten caught making home brew. The year was 1920 and Prohibition was newly in force. Henry didn't go along with the government telling a man when and if he could drink a little hooch.

    The two years Henry spent in jail was the only true freedom Catherin had since she married him five years before. *The stupid bastard thought I was pregnant then or he never would have settled for me. If only I hadn't gotten pregnant now everything* would be fine, nobody would dare tell him I was screwing around on him while he was locked up. When he does get out he'll probably beat the piss out of me and pull a rabbit, he ain't got nothing to hold him here now.

 Rolling over, very nearly smothering the sleeping infant who was tucked in the cot beside her, she faded off to a healing sleep and generous dreams.

 When she woke she lay still dreaming of a better time and place. Back home with Pa and Ma she'd had enough to eat and a roof over her head, never mind that she had to listen to the constant nagging about her lack of ambition around the farm. *Who the hell wants to pull a cow's tits every day of every week for the rest of her life. Ma's bitching about the way she hung the wash didn't help to make life easier either. Oh shit, there goes the kid wailing like a banshee. Probably wanting breakfast and my milk ain't started yet. Gotta figure out something for him to eat till I get some milk started. Can't afford to buy milk with the money I got coming in and there ain't any other work out there. Good he went back to sleep, he's gonna be a good baby, a little sweet heart.*

The restaurant, Ma's Home Cooking, where she worked had given her two days to recuperate and then she was expected back to work slinging hash. Goldie, the women who owned the joint knew her situation and had sympathy, but times were hard and business was business.

With cold fear in her heart Catherin counted the days until Henry would be released. Twenty two days and he would walk through that door and find her and a kid that was not his.

Again the child's crying brought her back from her reverie. Would she have milk for the child, she didn't know. Kneading her breast and getting nothing, she realized that she might never have enough milk to feed the child. Her eating habits were sporadic to say the least and money was always lacking. Putting her finger in between the small pink lips she let the child suck until he fell asleep.

Maybe Henry would accept the child if I'm especially good to him when he gets home. Christ what a damn fool I am thinking that. He's gonna kill me and the child. Maybe if I hid the kid with friends I could get away with keeping him alive. Tommy and Josie are the only ones I trust and they are poorer than me. If they would take the kid in I could slip them some money on the side and Henry would never know I'd betrayed him. No, she thought, That's not gonna work, Tommy is Henry's friend too and I know he'd slip and let the cat out of the bag. If only I had gotten out of town when he was first locked up I could be safe somewhere else, not shitting my pants cause he's coming home.

 Days ran into weeks and Catherin still hadn't solved her problem, where was she going to keep the kid when Henry got out? Every time she looked at the calender her instincts warned her to run, but she had nowhere to run to.

 It's almost time, he got out yesterday and spent his first day with his friend Tommy, drinking hooch and playing cards. He's sure to hear about the kid and he'll be walking through that door. My ass is gonna be in a sling for sure. Please God let him drop dead before he ever gets here.

 God wasn't listening.

 Maybe He is punishing me for screwing around while Henry was locked up.

My friend Josie said God ain't like that, but what the hell does she know?

Two month old Steven watched wide eyed and frozen as his mother was beaten by a man he'd never seen before. The man finally left after breaking every dish and piece of furniture in the apartment. Catherin lay bleeding on the glass littered floor until her friend Sally came to check on her and the kid. It took her a month to fully recover physically from the beating although the memory of the humiliation kept it fresh in her mind.

The apartment Catherin lived in was half a house and the owner, Frank Freeman, and his brow beaten wife, Hilda, lived in the other half. Frank was a puny little man with a million wrinkles, a tick in the right eye and a Napoleon Bonaparte attitude, he had convinced himself that all the women craved his attention. When Frank found out that Henry was not coming back, he coerced Catherin into sleeping with him in exchange for lower rent. With her part time job at Ma's Home Cooking, and the lower rent she was able to make ends meet and even eked out enough for a toy or two for that first

Christmas.

Her mother's protective instinct kicked in with a vengeance after *Henry left*. She worked hard, saved pennies, determined to survive even after being beaten nearly to death for having another mans child. She devoted herself to Steven and began calling him, Mama's little Sweet Boy.

When Steven was five years old he came home, nose bloody, clothes torn and a bruise on his forehead. When Catherin asked him what happened, he crawled into her lap and said that the kids teased him because he had such a funny name. They made fun of him and said that nobody named their kid Sweet Boy. Catherin explained to him that his name was Steven Boyd Gilbert but because she loves him so much she calls him her Sweet Boy.

Steven pouted and declared that he would not answer to Steven ever, ever again, from now on the only name he would ever answer to was Sweet Boy. He'd make the kids like it or else. He became a cynical old man at the age of five.

One afternoon after a heated game of kick the can Sweet Boy walked into the house and found his mother and a stranger sitting at the scared wooden table drinking coffee. Confusion flooded his heart and mind when he seen his mother laughing and flirting with that fat old man. Running to Catherin, he climbed into her lap, hugged her neck while he peeked out of the corner of his eyes at the man with the shiny bald head.

The man smiled and said, "Son, I'm your daddy, well not really, but I am married to your mom and I guess that counts for something."

His mother just sat there smiling and nodding her head. *What did that mean to him,* Sweet Boy silently questioned, *did he want me to hug him or shake hands, or what?*

Henry said that he had come home to his family, "your mother is getting tired of working and taking care of a kid all by herself. A women needs a man to help out with her other needs too." He smirked,

Sweet Boy didn't know what that man was talking about but he didn't trust him. He could smell the musty sweat from the man that his mother was acting so silly with. On her face was a foolish look that the boy had never seen before.

"Boy, I'm the man of the house now and you better get used to it. Go outside and play with your friends, me and your mother got some catching up to do."

The confused lad turned, looked into his mother's eyes and saw rejection for the first time in his young life. He was too young to realize that a grown women needs love and affection from more than a child of five, her mind and body was calling out for physical love and she planned on giving into temptation. Her hunger had never been gratified by the fumbling efforts of her landlord, Frank Freeman, and Henry was dammed good in bed.

Pushing Sweet Boy off her lap, she simpered at the man as she headed for the bedroom. Standing there dazed by his mother's rude dismissal the boy had his first lesson in competing with an adversary who seemed to be stealing his mother's affection.

Life became a nightmare for the boy, mother was always busy working or cooking food for that man who now lived with them. She didn't even look like the woman he had grown up with, she dyed her long brown hair a garish blond and wore big hook earrings that dangled down to her shoulders. Her mouth was a bright red slash in her sallow gray face. The fat ugly man was always saying mean dirty things to Mama and she would just giggle and shake her butt at him.

    Sweet Boy watched with feelings of emptiness. He was never included in their private little jokes and he felt alone and abandoned. It was as if he no longer existed in his mother's world. Many nights he sneaked out of the house and watched through the window. He knew It didn't matter if he did get caught, they never noticed him even when he was standing right in the same room with them.

     Frank Freeman continued to hang around and soon became fast friends with the man, they sat at the kitchen table and drank the stuff that the man was making in the metal wash tub. Sweet Boy had tasted it and it had a horrible taste but it did make the fat man happy. He didn't beat Mama as much after he had spent a day drinking with Mr. Freeman. When Mama came home they would all drink some of that stuff and then

Mr. Freeman and Mama would go out of the room for a while. Sweet Boy didn't want to think about where they were and what they were doing, but he knew it was bad because Mama always had tears in her eyes when she came back into the room.

    Mr. Freeman gave Sweet Boy a shoe shine box that his nephew had used before he ran away. Frank Freeman didn't know that his wife, Hilda, had given the boy her small stash of savings so the lad could get to his grand parent's home in Standish. It wasn't far to travel, but the boy would need extra money to convince the grandparents to take him in.

    Henry scowled and told Sweet Boy that now he had no excuse for shirking his duty. He should get his ass out and earn his keep.

    Sweet Boy was in his glory with the box and a chance to earn some money. The box was well built and someone had taken the time to design it well. He was able to sit on the slab of hard wood at the and of the box while shinning his customer's black patent leather shoes. Whoever built the box had even put a leather strap on it so he could carry it over his shoulder. Taking his shoe shine box early every mornings, Sweet Boy ran all the way to the center of town so he could catch the men who went to offices in the big white house on the top of the hill. They soon knew his name and treated him as though he was important to their day. They sometimes gave him two nickels for a shine instead of one, he was saving one nickel to get out of his mother's house and he bought a stick of licorice with the other. He had it all figured out, she'd never miss him and he wouldn't have to listen to the fat ass and his mean mouth anymore. The boy figured if he could save ten dollars in one chunk he could move into a place of his own. He was proud of himself for thinking up this plan, after all how many guys could say they were out on their own at the age of eight.

    Sweet Boy was growing into a a sturdy little fellow, with straight blond hair that was rarely cut and when it was cut it was hacked off by his mother, leaving a ragged mess, but his contagious smile kept his customers coming back to him for their shoes to be shined. Sweet Boy didn't have a real bed and most nights he slept on a sofa in the living room. He stayed outside until late at night so he didn't have to see and hear the antics of his mother and that man. He hated that sofa, it sagged in the middle and smelled of smoke and urine, but it was a place to lay his head.

Sweet Boy soon picked up on the off color language from the other boys who worked the streets and could rip off a line of curses with the best of them. He was careful not to slip when he was home with Mother, after all she was a lady.

Now, most of the time Mama wore a black eye or bruised face and the boy's gut would turn at the thought that his mother was being treated so badly. Why didn't she throw the fat ass out, he had never brought anything into the house except pain.

On Sunday mornings there was no need for Sweet Boy to hurry out to work, the offices down town were closed and most folks were going to church with their families, the boy would lay and pretend he was sleeping just so he could hear the soft murmur of his mother's voice. The boy knew his mother was working hard trying to better herself and her surroundings. One Sunday morning he heard her say she wanted to buy a linoleum to dress up the brown plank floors in the living room. The floors hadn't been scrubbed in years but nothing was ever mentioned about cleaning it and she never seemed to have the money for such a luxury as linoleum anyway. Lard Ass complained that the money would be better spent helping him with the new business he was thinking of starting. Neither plan ever worked out and the floor just kept getting dirtier.

    The fat man never went to work anywhere, he always seemed to be home watching the people in the neighborhood as they went about their day to day living. He delighted in verbally torturing Sweet Boy by referring to the boy's lack of a father. "Hey little bastard, come here little bastard, shine my shoes, and make sure you don't use spit to make em shine. I don't even want the spit from you, being a bastard might be catching." The fat man never bothered to take baths and Sweet Boy hated to even get near him much less give the lard ass his spit.

    A banging on their door early one morning shook the whole household awake. The sheriff pushed his way in, grabbed Henry by the arm, twisted it up behind his back and pushed his rotund body to the floor.

He made a humorous picture for Sweet Boy to enjoy, fat, white ass hanging out of the opening in the rear of his once clean white long johns. His sweaty bald head shinning under the light that hung from the ceiling on a twisted brown cord. The boy knew he would never forget the picture of Lard Ass's groveling humiliation. Pinching his cheeks to keep from laughing out loud, Sweet Boy savored every moment of Henry's altercation with the sheriff.

Henry whined that the sheriff had disturbed him, a hard working man who was trying to rest on his day off. He shouted that the sheriff 's man handling folks was against the law and he would see to it that he was punished for it. He had friends in high places and they would see that the sheriff might even lose his job.

Sheriff Lennard Dennis laughed and twisted a little harder. "I got me a couple of bindle stiffs that say you cheated them out of a dollar. They say you sold them rot gut instead of shine, can't do that, it ain't gonna happen in my town. We're law abiding folks around here and you don't cheat yer neighbors."

Sweet Boy watched as Lard Ass, the so called big man begged for a chance to make it right, he'd give them back their money and a bottle of the good stuff to boot.

"See that you do and don't let me hear of another complaint or back to jail you go. I don't know why that good women of your's keeps you around," said the sheriff as he let Henry up.

While walking to the door shaking his head he mumbled,"Never understand it, never in this lifetime."

The boy, who was watching the whole episode had to agree with the sheriff. He couldn't understand it either.

Oh shit, he thought, I better get my ass out of here while the sheriff is still out front otherwise I'll get my ass busted. Lard Ass is gonna have to take his temper out on somebody and sure as hell that somebodies me. Sweet Boy grabbed his fishing pole and headed toward the Saginaw River. Last night Freddie the finch and Brain said they were catching perch and the fish were still biting when they had to leave.

Freddie the finch got his knick name because he was always whistling, you could hear him before you could see him. Sweet Boy wondered what the hell Freddie had to be happy about, his dad was dead, his sister was an imbecile that all the older boys screwed, and Freddie himself had rotted buck teeth, and ears that stuck out like the handles on a jug. Sweet Boy always felt lucky when he was with Freddie. Maybe that was what the poor fool was so happy about, he had friends.

    Brain got his knick name because he loved big words and used them when ever he wanted to attract attention. The fact that Brain was the tenth child of Herb and Donna Schultz seemed to Sweet Boy, to be the ideal place. Folks said the Schultz mother and father spent all their time in bed that's why they had so many kids, but Sweet Boy knew that Mrs. Schultz sewed for the towns folk and Herb had a big garden and a Black Smith shop. They both were always working every time he visited. Their kids were always well dressed and fed, what more could you ask ? He wished he had been born to the Schultz family then he would have brothers and sisters too.

Sweet Boy had to chuckle when he remembered the first time he experienced Brain's habit of using unusual words to build himself up. Freddie the Finch and two or three Hobos were hunched over a low fire watching a fry pan full of bacon cook. Somebody had scored a slab of side pork and they were sharing it with the few guys that were there. Brain rushed up face flushed, eyes filled with delight and shouted, "I saw them, I saw them just now. They were out behind Frankel's barn and they were copulating right there in front of God and everybody who wanted to see."

'Who,? …..Who was out behind the barn doing what ever that is?" Freddie The Finch asked."What the hell is copulating? "

"It's fucking," one of the hobos answered.

"Ya, its screwing," another of the hobos chimed in.

"Then why the hell didn't he say so? I get so tired of his shit. Big words don't change the answer, it just makes it harder to understand." Freddie the Finch sputtered as he was stood over Brain with his face almost touching the other boy. "Brain," he said, " you gotta quit that shit or don't hang out with me no more. You don't need big words to be my friend."

"Son, there's some folks need a gaff to help them get noticed. I'm afraid your buddy here is one of those people." The hobo, called Martin said as he wiped the grease out of his shaggy gray beard. "He's harmless, but I must admit he is a pain in the butt. Now lets finish eating before it get cold."

"Well, I still want to know who was out there screwing." pouted Freddie.

"It was the Widow Brown and Miss Ida's husband," Smirked Brain. "There's gonna hell when Miss Ida finds out."

"How's she gonna find out? I ain't gonna tell and you better not tell either." Sweet Boy grumbled. "Somehow we'd be likely to get the blame no matter what."

Clyde, taking the pan off the fire, had to agree with his young friend's prediction. Clyde too had been on the wrong end of a bad situation and was nearly hung for it. After divvying up the bacon and a loaf of bread they all sat down to eat and contemplate the gossip that Brain had brought to the camp.

To Sweet Boy it seemed like his stomach was always empty. Often the hobo's at the camp let him cook his fish over their fire if he would divvy up with them. Mother didn't seem to cook anymore and a growing boy needs food.

   He had spent this particular Sunday catching fish, cooking them and eating till his stomach could hold no more. His second favorite past time was sharing stories and lies with the hobos who were camped by the river. Sweet Boy told one of the traveling men, "This is a pretty good life for a young guy like you if your alone in this world, If I didn't have obligations I'd join you, but I'm not alone, I got a Mother to watch over even if I can't do much right now, I can still be there."

   "That prick of a boyfriend, husband, or whatever the hell he is, still there? Want me to tune him up for you?" Asked Clyde, the biggest, toughest hobo, "I could teach him a lesson he won't forget."

   Sweet Boy answered, "He'd just take it out on me and my mother when you are gone. Clyde you're big enough to kick his ass but I gotta grow a couple more years before I can. Some day I'll be big enough and strong enough to kick his ass, in the mean time my stash is growing and me and her can get away from that bastard."

Sweet Boy flexed the muscle in his right arm showing the beginnings of a well developed eight year old boy.

"Son, yer right but I wouldn't want to tangle ass with you when yer growed . I learned early on that it is foolhardy to tangle ass with a small man, they never give up, every time you turn around their climbing yer frame. They hang on like a rat terrier with his jaws locked on yer ass. But it's up to you kid.

I left that same shit behind about ten years ago. I lit out and I ain't been back. Heard the old man died a while back and Ma remarried, so there's no reason to go back now."

Folks in town called the men who rode the rails, bums,drifters, hobos, and beggars, but to the boys who hung out at the river they were friends and teachers. Sweet Boy had heard one of the hobos call himself a knight of the road. That is exactly how Sweet Boy thought of them, especially Clyde. Sure they went from door to door asking for food but his friends had never hurt anybody. They just went away peacefully when the home owner said no. They drifted from town to town looking for work but always seemed to end up back here at the river. Sweet Boy liked to think they missed him as much as he missed them. They were like family.

    When the campfire died down and the drifters began to yawn, stretch, and fade into the dark comfort of the night, Sweet Boy knew it was time to head home.

    Peeking through the stained glass window in the door, Sweet Boy hoped to see an empty chair by the table, but no luck. There was Fat Ass slouched in his usual place drinking the slop he made out of corn.

    As soon as he was old enough to explore Sweet Boy had found a safe refuge under the front porch that wrapped around the front of the house. It sagged in the middle from lack of support, but it was still safer then being in the same room with Henry. Sweet Boy crawled into his hidy hole and checked his bank, counting the nickels that he had saved. The bank was an old fruit jar and in it was the treasures of his life time, a sling shot that Clyde had made for him to hunt rabbits with, a sum of three dollars and fifty cents, and a ladies handkerchief that still smelled like the women who gave it to him to wipe the sweat off his brow.

Sweet Boy lay thinking off the story mother had told him about how they ended up in this town, this place. He wondered if there were any other way to live. It seemed as though the people he met when he was shinning shoes always seemed happy and kind, did they really feel that way or were they pretending like he did when he was away from the house.

The porch was a ramshackle addition built after a house fire had nearly destroyed the main building. Miner repairs had been done on the house by Frank Freeman, but like everything else he had ever done it looked like it was repaired by a wood butcher. Nothing was completely finished before he moved on to the next project. Frank was in a hurry to get the house fixed up so he could rent half to help pay for the repairs and give him a steady income.

Henry Gilbert was the first and only one that came to see the rental that had posted on the tree in the middle of town. Frank was in his glory. Finally he had some one to share the expenses. Henry said he didn't give a shit that they had to share the same outhouse with Frank and his wife, just don't expect him or Catherin to clean it.

 Mother said her heart nearly stopped when she seen where they were going to live but Henry assured her that they would be moving up in the world when he got his business started. After four years of broken promises, Mother knew they would never be anything but white trash selling homemade hooch. When she had first gotten her job at, Ma's Home Cooking, she had her hopes renewed by the way she was treated by Goldie, her boss, and the patrons who ate there regularly.

 In the meantime Henry had gotten caught making moonshine and was been locked up in the jail waiting for the judge to sentence him. He was even more miserable than usual and Catherin hated going to visit him in the jail but she had to or else he would make her pay when he got out.

 Mama said a year was a long time to go with out a man to ease some of the loneliness, so she had become close to another young fellow while Henry was away. She told him a little bit about his real father and Sweet Boy wondered if he ever went looking and found the man would the man take Sweet Boy in and love him like the Schultz's loved their kids.

    In reality, his father was a young fellow who sold tea and coffee to the local eateries. He had made an impression on Catherin from the first time he had walked through the front door. He complimented her, teased her and flirted with the now flustered Catherin until he walked out the door and left her with an empty feeling in her gut. He had said he would see her next month when he came back through town. She hoped he would keep his promise.

    When Jeffery, the sales man came back into town and found out Catherin was now alone he pursued her with a gentle passion that she had never experienced. Catherin surrendered to Jeffery's engaging charm and was soon deeply involved in an affair that gave her great pleasure. The imminent fear of being caught was always hanging over her head and heart. She had never been a chaste girl but this was different, she was in love.

When she realized that she was three months pregnant she hurried to the hotel where Jeffery had taken a room, finding it empty she left a note telling him of her good news. Believing that he would be as happy as she was she went to work and spent the day waiting on her steady costumers, smiling, humming and floating on a cloud of joy.

When Goldie asked why she was so happy today Catherin swore her to secrecy and told her the news.

"Honey, yer shitting me, and yer happy about this predicament, girl he's got a whole passel of girls he's screwing every time he comes to town. Didn't you ever notice how my business picks up when he comes to town, he's keeping half the women in this town satisfied."

"Well," Catherin declared in defense of Jeffery, "when he finds out about his baby he'll stop that screwing around and stick with me. I can leave Henry! Jeffery, me, and the baby can be together."

"Ya well, you keep on believing that and

the moon is made out of green cheese." Shaking her head in disbelief Goldie went back to work in the kitchen and all the folks in the dinning area heard was the slamming of pans. Goldie liked this girl Catherin but she was afraid the girl headed down the wrong track and she knew Jeffery would get rid of her fast now that she was in the family way. She would just become a mill stone around his neck.

Catherin never seen Jeffery again.

He had gone back to his room, read the note, packed his bag and was gone before the sun set.

The next month a strange sales man showed up at the diner, introduced himself and told them that he would be taking over Jeffery's route, now that Jeffery had transferred to another area.

Catherin was heart broken, she had secretly dreamed that Jeffery had gone to get his affairs straightened out and that he would be back to take her away from all this. When she finally accepted the fact that Jeffery was a cad and philander she felt her hope for a better life drift from her heart. Her guts rolled, she felt dizzy, she wondered about the old stories of lost loves and how folks pined away until they died. If it were really true could she be love sick or was it just gas?

The rest of her pregnancy went smoothly and she soon was so big that she could hardly push herself up to the shelf where she picked up the trays of hot food to serve to the customers. Her steady customers often teased her that she was having two for the price of one. She prayed fervently that they were wrong, she wasn't even sure she was going to keep this one, but who the hell would take on another mouth to feed in these had times. The fact that her husband had been gone Two years and could not be the father was also influencing her decision.

Mama had explained to Sweet Boy how she had fallen in love with him, her baby, when she first saw him and felt a fierce determination to protect him at all cost. The boy knew that she spoke the truth because for the first few years of his life he was wrapped in mother's love.

Chapter Two

Late one Saturday night after a full day of shinning shoes and fetching news papers for his customers Sweet Boy walked into the house and there was his mother lying on the dilapidated couch bleeding from her mouth and nose, her arm was twisted at an unusual angle and tears were streaming down her face. Running to his mother Sweet Boy demanded to know what happened. He already knew, but he wanted Mother to say it out loud.

"Your mother fell down," Smirked lard ass, "she's so dammed clumsy it's a wonder she didn't break her neck. Maybe next time she will."

There sat Henry, his hands and shirt bloody, daring Catherin to say any different.

His mother agreed with her abuser, saying, "I'll be all right in the morning, I just can't seem to walk down steps without falling. Baby, please get me a cold wet rag to stop my nose bleed."

"You don't need to be making a mess around here with bloody rags. Your nose bleed will stop pretty soon or else you'll bleed to death, either way you will stop bleeding." Henry leered at Catherin and added, "Don't pretend your arm is hurt so you don't have to go to work, we need the money you make for supplies. You will work tomorrow no excuses. "

Sweet Boy crept out of the house while his mother's husband unleashed an other torrent of verbal abuse on the beaten down figure of Catherin while she cringed in the corner of the sofa.

Running to the sheriff's house, Sweet boy pounded on the door until it was answered by the sheriff's wife. "Son, what the hell are you doing waking me out of a sound sleep. What do you want?"

"That asshole Henry is beating on my mother again. He's going to kill her! Where's the sheriff, I need him to come with me."

"Sheriff is gone till tomorrow, come back then." Slamming the door, the women stood behind the lace curtains watching the boy dejectedly make his way back to the only place he could call home. *Too bad that mother ain't got the sense she was born with and kick that free loader out on his lazy ass.* Thought Mrs. Dennis, *Oh well, ain't my problem, some women will do anything to have a man in their bed.*

Thank God I got me a decent man, he ain't much to look at but he does work and he's good to me. Yawning and scratching her huge round breast she crawled back into her soft warm bed.

Sweet Boy hurried back to the house fearing to find out that the ass hole had done more damage while he was gone. The lights were out and he could hear mother and lard ass talking low, then the rhythm of the bed started just as if nothing had happened.

"God damn her, how could she after all the shit he gives her? Well I'm done worrying about her. She can just go to hell!"

He now was having a hard time remembering that safe, warm, love that he knew in the beginning but a faint memory of Mother's tenderness still lingered some where in his soul.

Nature has a way of erasing horror that is too much for a young child to bear. Deep sleep helps to drain the initial terror, dulling the pain that remembering brings. Sweet Boy had all the anger and pain that a small boy could absorb and still stay sane. The sobbing child lay down on the filthy sofa, rolled over, continued sniffling until he was fast asleep.

Waking earlier than usual, Sweet Boy grabbed his shine box and sneaked out of the house. The last thing he heard from the bedroom was loud snoring and Henry farting. He knew it was Henry because he always gave a contented, "Ah,"when he was done.

Heading toward town he met up with Freddie the Finch and was informed that there wasn't any sense in going to work as the bank was closed and no one was working today.

"What the hell is going on?" asked sweet Boy.

"Don't know, Pop said there was a run on the bank and the president ran away with the money. I guess he's still running. Pop don't care cause we never did have any money in the bank anyhow. What little Pop has is under his mattress. Can't nobody steal it from there."

"Come on," said Freddie, "lets go down to the river and have a pissing contest, maybe some one else besides Brain will win it this time."

"Ya know Brain's gonna win, his pecker is the biggest and he always wins . Wait till I get my pole. We can catch our lunch and stay the day."

The picture they made that day will remain indelibly written on the pages of time. Two boys eight and eleven, fishing poles slung over slim shoulders, coveralls dusty from the dry, dead earth around them, straw hats sitting jauntily on uncombed hair, and a barefoot bounce to their step.

Spitting chew to see who could spit the furtherest was another of their favorite pastimes, but they couldn't always talk their friends the hobos out of their precious Skoal. The pissing contest was the easiest, they always had a lot of piss, cause water filled the gut when you're hungry and the fish weren't biting.

Not many hobos were down at the river and the few that were there didn't seem too friendly. Sweet Boy and Freddie went further down the banks of the river and sat close to the brush that lined the river bank. The boys had an instinct about the strangers that rode the rail and that instinct was warning them that these guys were up to no good.

"Best to keep our distance," warned Freddie the Finch and Sweet Boy was only too glad to accept the warning from the older boy. They fished, goofed around with fishing poles pretending they were having duels, climbed trees, but something was missing. The joyous feeling of freedom was gone for both boys.

The day was getting cool, the sun had gone behind heavy clouds and the air smelled of rain. Freddie the Finch always had to be home if it rained as his mother was afraid of storms and his father was dead, so it was Freddie's job to be there for her.

Sweet Boy didn't want to go home yet but he didn't want to stay by the river alone and Brain didn't come as he usually did after supper, so the down hearted boy slowly made his way home to the last place in the world he really wanted to be. As he drew closer to the house his dread grew. What hell would Lard Ass have planned for him or his mother tonight. He had all day to drink and think up something mean spirited and down right evil to torture them with.

It was too quiet in the house, had mother ran away from the fat ass or stayed at work hoping that animal would leave them alone. No she wouldn't leave me to face him alone, she must be there in the bedroom or maybe she's in the out house hiding.

    Sweet Boy sneaked around the side of the house, crept up to the outhouse and quietly knocked on the side of the small building, no answer, he rapped again and whispered his mother's name. Still no answer. He hesitated to open the door in case someone was in there but he couldn't wait any longer and fear forced him to pull the door open. No one there, but the stench was over powering, he felt his stomach roll and he threw himself as far away as he could from the reeking building and into the wet grass near by. Where could she be?

    Forcing himself to go to the front door he held his hand to his forehead and peered through the dusky window in the wooden door. There was Henry sitting in his usual place but something new was added. The rusty old shovel was leaning against the wall near his chair and there was dirt on the floor around it.

    Sweet Boy pushed open the door and stepped into the kitchen just as Henry drank the last of his brew from a glass jar. "Hey little bastard, yer home just in time to fill my jug for me and this time don't spill a drop. Can't waste good shine cause yer clumsy like yer ma."

The silence was eerie, where was Mother? She was always home by now, she didn't dare be late or he'd pound on her. Something funny was going on, I gotta figure out what he's done with her.

"Where's Ma, ain't she home yet?"

"She ain't coming home, I kicked her ass out, she ain't much good around here anyway. Don't never clean this rat hole and all she cooks is slop. She couldn't cook shit for a beggar. Get your ass to bed you're gonna have to work more hours and earn more then you been making. Oh, by the way, while I was digging under the porch for worms I found your stash, three dollars and fifty five cents. Ain't much but I can use it to buy corn. That sure is a tight fit under there I nearly didn't make it out."

Henry sat caressing the shovel that stood next to his chair.

A rage tore through Sweet Boy's small body, he began shaking but not from fear this time. All the pent up anger he had buried was coming to the surface and it felt so good. He could visualize killing Fat Ass, dragging his ugly body out into the yard, spitting on it and leaving it out there for all the world to see. He was so lost in the dream he did indeed attack the beast that had treated his mother so badly. Fist flying, eyes wild, he hit the man twice before the object of his rage realized that Sweet Boy was intent on killing him. Henry laughed crazily put his hand on Sweet boy's forehead and held his small attacker away at arms length. The furious boy continued to swing at the object of his rage until running out of steam he fell to the floor. Henry kicked the boy in the ass several times forcing him to crawl to the door. When he had reached the door Henry picked him up by his shirt and threw him out into the yard.

    After lying in the dirt for a better part of an hour Sweet Boy dragged himself under the porch, gathered what was left of his treasures and headed for the river.

    When he reached the only place he now felt safe he sat and thought about the scene he had just left. Fat Ass never dug worms for him before, why would he start now? Where was Mother and how was he going to get the sheriff to look for her?

As he sat pondering these questions, Freddie the Finch and Brain came strolling down the trail through the trees toward their favorite fishing spot. When they spotted their friend sitting near the burnt out fire instead of fishing they knew something was wrong and like all good friends they came running.

"What happened why aren't you fishing," asked Freddie?

"Shut up!"Shouted Brain, "can't you see something is really wrong?"

" Well sure I can see," retorted Freddie, "but I want to know what's going on."

"Shut yer pie hole and listen," whispered Freddie.

"My mother's disappeared, Lard Ass says he threw her out but I don't believe him. Something has happened to her." Sweet Boy fought the temptation to cry. Changing the subject might keep him from looking like a baby in front of his friends. "Today is my birthday and she wouldn't leave on my birthday. That bastard stole the money I was saving in my treasure jar under the porch. I don't care about the money so long as I can find my mother. I think he did something to her. He had the shovel in the house by him. He said he was digging worms but he never did that before. I just gotta find her first before I decide what to do."

"We'll help you look," offered Freddie, and Brain silently nodded his head. "How old are you now," asked Brain, "Are you eleven just like me or are you ten?"

"I'm ten today," Sweet Boy lied, he couldn't let his friends see him as a baby.

"I know mother would be here for my birthday, she is always here on my birthday" Sniffled Sweet Boy, trying to hold back the tears.

After much discussion they settled on a plan of action, Brain would go to all the people that might take her in, Freddie would search around the house for any spots where she might be hiding, and Sweet Boy would search the area for any place that there was fresh dirt or digging. Brain had argued with Sweet Boy, he didn't want his friend to find the body of his mother. Brain had lost the argument and was secretly glad.

"Don't let Lard Ass catch you," Sweet Boy warned as they went their separate ways.

In the distance the boys could hear the train whistle crying out in the clear fall air, a mournful feeling stole into Sweet Boy's heart. It was as if the whistle was dolefully delivering the sad tidings, *she's gone, she's gone.*

They searched most of the day and found nothing. Meeting back at the river at dusk they informed the new hobos that had come in on the coal train, what they were doing. Two of the newcomers had offered to help but the others said it was not their problem and didn't want to be involved..

Sitting around the campfire the search party discussed where they had looked and where they would look as soon as it got light.

Davey, one of the friendly hobos, asked if they had searched under the porch, he suggested that Lard Ass sounds as though he doesn't move around too much and suggested that no one would look under there now that Sweet Boy's hiding place was discovered.

A sinking feeling filled Sweet Boy's gut, Davey's right, Henry hardly ever leaves the house unless it's to buy supplies. He guards that still like it was gold. he would never go far from the house unless he was forced to. Besides, thought Sweet Boy, He's too lazy to carry mother's body any farther then he had to.

"Dear God don't let my mother be dead, she's all I got." The boy silently prayed. Jumping up tears streaming down his face Sweet Boy started toward the path to his house. Davey sensing the danger the boy would run into if he challenged his step father, grabbed him and held him in a bear hug, holding the frantic boy Davey coaxed him back to the fire. Davey patiently explained to the child who sat frozen with fear and anger, that he wouldn't be able to search very well at night and even if he did find something he would have to wait until morning to do anything about it. Sweet Boy pretended to agree and sat huddled near the smoldering ashes of the fire. Waiting until all the others had found their place of rest for the night, Sweet Boy lay shivering as the fall night crept in and covered the boy with bone chilling dew. It was as if nature was purifying the child with its tears in preparation for the days ahead.

When Sweet Boy heard the snores

coming from the brush surrounding the camp fire he knew the hobos were fast asleep and he could leave without argument or opposition.

    Leaving his fishing pole where it was propped up against a tree, the boy slipped out of the camp and headed toward the only house that he had ever known. He couldn't call it a home because a home is where you are supposed to feel safe and loved and he had felt neither from that run down shack that had housed him for the past eight years.

    Making his way back to the house in the dark was proving more difficult than he had expected. Trees that were his friends in the heat of the day became eerie looming shapes in the black hours before dawn. The uneven path that was formed by small feet making numerous trips to the river became treacherous clods of earth pulling at hesitant feet. The sounds that surrounded him while he pushed his way through this suddenly unfamiliar woods were strange and unrelated to anything he had ever remembered hearing. Panic set in. He ran as though his life was in jeopardy from the legendary evil spirits that every boy knows haunts the woods at night.

Bursting out of the woods he bumped into the outhouse that sat behind the house. The familiar odor of human body waste gave him a vague sense of comfort. He knew where he was now, everything came back into focus. The light in the house called to him and he responded by peeking through the window into the empty kitchen.

Where was he, what has he done with mother and why is the shovel gone? Pulling the squeaky door open, Sweet Boy stepped into the room and felt as though he was being wrapped in a invisible blanket of warmth. Suddenly he knew, *she's dead, Mother is dead and that bastard killed her. I have got to find her body so I can prove it to the sheriff.*

Going into the back room where that ass hole's tub of rot gut stood in the corner, Sweet boy struggled with the heavy half filled container. Tipping the liquid onto the floor he went to the knife drawer and poked a hole in the tub with a sharp knife. A feeling of satisfaction stole over him. Now he had to find Mother's body and give that killer his just deserts. Grabbing his shine box he headed toward the door just as Henry came staggering through the opening.

Henry lifted his head and smelled the foul air that permeated the house.

"You little bastard, you son of a whore. You're asking for the same thing your mother got, laying in her own shit, that same shit she made when she shit you out. I'm just the guy to give it to you too."

Reaching out toward Sweet Boy, Henry slipped on the wet floor, clumsily fell into the puddle of booze that had seeped into the kitchen. The alcohol lay pooling near the front door.

This was Sweet Boy's chance to escape! He made a dash for the back door and flew back out into the black night. He lay shaking in a patch of scrub brush that grew near the path to the outhouse, he could smell the small house that held their excrement and his mind went back to the last thing Lard Ass had said.

No, he thought, *he couldn't be that evil. No one is that vicious.* But he knew in his heart that his mother's resting place was at the bottom of the outhouse. Now all he had to do was prove it.

Waiting for daylight was the most difficult thing that Sweet Boy had ever done, but he knew if he went to the sheriff's office before daylight no one would be there and the sheriff didn't like being woken before seven o'clock on a week day. Crawling under the porch into his snug hideaway, he waited. Gone were his feeling of tranquility as he lay in his once snug little hollowed out nest. A feeling of fear penetrated his shivering little body. *Gotta get out of here,* beat in his brain, *Run, s*aid his heart but the child couldn't listen. He had to find out what happened to his mother first, then he would think about protecting himself. Dosing off was the first mistake Sweet Boy made, next was when he crawled out from under the sagging porch without checking to see if the coast was clear. He never saw the shovel being swung directly at him, he dropped down dead from the terrible blow.

Freddie the Finch, who had just come searching for his friend Sweet Boy, saw it all so he was next, he hadn't realized what had just happened until it was too late. The out of control maniac swung the shovel at the paralyzed boy and caught him along side the head, it split open like a ripe melon. Henry had waited, scheming in his booze warped mind to rid himself of wife and child in one felled blow and his demented thoughts told him that one more would be alright. He could always say that the two boys had killed Catherin and then they had run away. His whiskey soaked mind urged him to drag the bodies to the river and let the water wash away his crimes.

Grabbing the boys by the back of their collars, he dragged them toward the river. Huffing and puffing he struggled through the underbrush until he reached the train bridge, there he sat down and tried to catch his breath. Pains tore their way through his chest, his eyes lost focus, and his last thoughts were, I *shouldn't have dragged the little bastards this far.*

The whole town was aghast at the events on this fatal Friday in 1931, the bank had failed, the bank president had shot himself, the disappearance of a local mother, and the murder of two boys down by the river. One of the boys stepfather had found the bodies and had suffered a heart attack. *Poor man must have gone into shock,* the towns folk whispered.

How could this happen in such a friendly small town like Bay City Michigan, without folks suspecting that something was very wrong?

The hobos had suddenly disappeared from along the river, they knew who would be blamed for everything that had happened, and they were right.

The gossips in the town were kept busy for months telling the tale of the two murdered boys and the women who went missing on the day the boys were killed. Did the missing mother kill the boys and if so, why?

However many of the town folks claimed the hobos had done the deed. The unsung hero of the tale was Henry, the man who some folks believed had died trying to save the boys from those murderous hobos.

The sheriff's wife kept her mouth closed and locked, she didn't want anyone to know that she had sent one of the unfortunate boys away.

The men in the town said nothing as they didn't want the world to know that they were Henry's best customers.

Frank Freeman's house mysteriously burned to the ground and he died trying to save it, his only valued possession. He was caught in the back draft while his wife, Hilda Freeman, watched stone faced. After the fire she moved to Standish to live with her parents and a nephew. The burnt ruins of the Freeman house was abandoned and the old outhouse caved in on its self, never to be used again.

    Five years later Brain Schultz jumped off the train bridge and drowned. Folks say that Brain Schultz never got over the death of his friends and his poor warped brain had become addled by the horror of their deaths. He kept claiming that Sweet Boy's father had killed the two boys. That poor boy just couldn't accept the fact that his friends were killed by the hobos.

    Brain's parents packed up the rest of their kids and household goods, left town, never to be seen again.

The End Ŏ

Somewhere on a lonely path near the river in Bay City, Michigan is a plot of ground where nothing grows, not grass, nor weeds, but every so often the bare earth spits up clean white pieces of bone. They lay like polished ivory on the dust covered earth, beckoning to be gathered up and given a place of permanence. Legend says these pieces of bone bring bad luck. No one ever collects them.

Folks who live near the place where all these events took place say if you go through the trees toward the river on a warm spring day and if you listen very carefully you may hear childish laughter floating on the breeze, followed by the faint echoes of whistling.

BN

Sweet Boy captured my heart and soul and I could not in good conscious let his short life go un-championed. The flat, bleak announcement of his murder did not provide any clue to the quality of his short life. No man should pass through our lives without leaving any essence, a flavor of their life, a subtle touch, an effect of our being touched by them.

It became my job to give Sweet Boy a name, a history, rare moments when he and his friends shared the beauty of the river, the glory of the fall leaves, nature's promise of change and renewal, and most important of all, hope for the reader.

B. N.